Friedrich von der Trenck

The Life of Baron Frederic Trenck

Containing his adventures, his cruel and excessive sufferings, during ten years

imprisonment, at the fortress of Magdeburg by command of the late King of

Prussia; also anecdotes, historical, political, and personal

Friedrich von der Trenck

The Life of Baron Frederic Trenck
*Containing his adventures, his cruel and excessive sufferings, during ten years imprisonment,
at the fortress of Magdeburg by command of the late King of Prussia; also anecdotes,
historical, political, and personal*

ISBN/EAN: 9783744797252

Printed in Europe, USA, Canada, Australia, Japan

More available books at **www.hansebooks.com**

THE

LIFE

OF

on Frederic Trenck;

CONTAINING

S ADVENTURES;

UEL AND EXCESSIVE SUFFERINGS, DUR-
NG TEN YEARS IMPRISONMENT, AT
THE FORTRESS OF MAGDEBURG,
BY COMMAND OF THE LATE

NG OF PRUSSIA;

ALSO,

NECDOTES,

ORICAL, POLITICAL, AND PERSONAL.

Translated from the German,

THOMAS HOLCROFT.

VOL. II.

LONDON:

ED FOR G. G. J. AND J. ROBINSON,
IN PATERNOSTER-ROW.

MDCCLXXXVIII.

THE

LIFE

OF

BARON TRENCK.

My dungeon was in a casemate, the fore part of which, six feet wide, and ten feet long, was divided by a party wall. In the inner wall were two doors, and a third at the entrance of the casemate itself. The window, in the seven feet thick wall, was so situated that, though I had light, I could see neither heaven nor earth; I could only see the roof of the magazine; within and without this window were iron bars, and in the space between an iron grating, so close, and so situated, by the rising of the walls, that it was impossible I should see any person without the prison, or that any person should see me. On the outside was a wooden palisadoe, six feet from the wall, by which the centinels were prevented from conveying any thing to me. I had a matrass, and a bedstead, but which was immoveably ironed to the floor, so that it was impossible I should drag it, and stand up to the window; beside the door was a small iron stove and a night table, in like manner fixed to the floor. I was not yet put in irons, and my allowance was a pound and a half per day of ammunition bread, and a jug of water.

From

From my youth I had always had a good appetite, and my bread was so mouldy I could scarcely at first eat the half of it. This was the consequence of Major Rieding's avarice, who endeavoured to profit even by this, so great was the number of unfortunate prisoners; therefore, it is impossible I should describe to my readers the excess of tortures that, during eleven months, I felt from ravenous hunger. I could, easily, every day have devoured six pounds of bread; and every twenty-four hours after having received, and swallowed, my small portion, I continued as hungry as before I began, yet must wait another twenty-four hours for a new morsel. How willingly would I have signed a bill of exchange for a thousand ducats, on my property at Vienna, only to have satiated my hunger on dry bread! For, so extreme

 was

was it, that, scarcely had I dropt into a sweet sleep, before I dreamed I was feasting at some table, luxuriously loaded, where, eating like a glutton, the whole company were astonished to see me, while my imagination was heated by the sensation of famine. Awakened by the pains of hunger, the dishes vanished, and nothing remained but the reality of my distress ; the cravings of nature were but inflamed, my tortures prevented sleep, and, looking into futurity, the cruelty of my fate suffered, if possible, increase, from imagining that the prolongation of pangs like these was insupportable. God preserve every honest man from sufferings like mine ! They were not to be endured by the villain most obstinate. Many have fasted three days, many have suffered want for a week, or more, but, certainly, no one, be-

sides

fides myfelf, ever endured it in the fame excefs for eleven months. Some have fuppofed that to eat little might become habitual, but I have experienced the contrary. My hunger increafed every day, and, of all the trials of fortitude my whole life has afforded, this, of eleven months, was the moft bitter.

Petitions, remonftrances, were of no avail; the anfwer was — " We muft " give no more, fuch is the king's " command." The Governor General Borck, born the enemy of man, re-plied, when I entreated, at leaft, to have my fill of bread, " You have " feafted often enough out of the " fervice of plate taken from the " king, by Trenck, at the battle " of Sorau ; you muft now eat " ammunition bread in your dirty " kennel. Your Emprefs makes no " allowance for your maintenance,

B 3   " and

" and you are unworthy of the bread
" you eat, or the trouble taken
" about you." Judge, reader, what
pangs such insolence, added to such
sufferings, must inflict. Judge what
were my thoughts, foreseeing, as I
did, an endless duration to this imprisonment, and these torments.

My three doors were kept ever
shut, and I was left to such meditations as such feelings, and such
hopes, might inspire. Daily, about
noon, once in twenty four hours,
my pittance of bread and water
was brought. The keys of all the
doors were kept by the governor;
the inner door was not opened, but
my bread and water were delivered
through an aperture. The prison
doors were opened only once a week,
on a Wednesday, when the governor,
and town major, my hole having
been first cleaned, paid their visit.

Having

IIaving remained thus two months, and obferved this method was invariable, I began to execute a projeﬆ I had formed, of the poﬃbility of which I was convinced.

Where the night-table and ﬆove ﬆood the floor was bricked, and this paving extended to the wall that feparated my cafemate from the adjoining one, in which was no prifoner. My window was only guarded by a fingle centinel; I, therefore, foon found, among thofe who fucceﬃvely relieved guard, two kind hearted fellows, who defcribed to me the fituation of my prifon; hence I perceived I might effeﬆ my efcape, could I but penetrate into the adjoining cafemate, the door of which was not ﬁhut. Provided I had a friend, and a boat waiting for me at the Elbe, or could I fwim acrofs

that

that river, the confines of Saxony were but a mile diftant.

To defcribe my plan, at length, would lead to prolixity, yet, I muft enumerate fome of its circum-ftances, as it was remarkably intri-cate, and of gigantic labour.

I worked through the iron, eigh-teen inches long, by which the night-table was faftened, and broke off the clinchings of the nails, but preferved their heads, that I might put them again in their places, and all might appear fecure to my weekly vifitors. This procured me tools to raife up the brick floor, under which I found earth. My firft attempt was to work a hole through the wall, feven feet thick, behind, and concealed by, the night-table. The firft layer was of brick. I afterwards came to large hewn ftones. I endeavoured, accu-

rately,

rately, to number and remember the bricks, both of the flooring and the wall, fo that I might replace them, and all might appear fafe. This having accomplifhed, I proceeded.

The day preceding vifitation all was carefully replaced, and the intervening mortar as carefully preferved; the whole had, probably, been whitewafhed a hundred times; and, that I might fill up all remaining interftices, I pounded the white ftuff this afforded, wetted it, made a brufh of my hair, then applied this plaifter, wafhed it over, that the colour might be uniform, and, afterward, ftripped myfelf, and fat, with my naked body againft the place, by the heat of which it was dried.

While labouring, I placed the ftones and bricks upon my bedftead, and, had they taken the precaution to come at any other time in the

 week,

week, the stated Wednesday excepted, I had, inevitably, been discovered; but, as no such ill accident befel me, in six months my Herculean labours gave me a prospect of success.

Means were to be found to remove the rubbish from my prison; all of which, in a wall so thick, it was impossible to replace: mortar and stone could not be removed. I, therefore, took the earth, scattered it about my chamber, and ground it under my feet the whole day, till I had reduced it to dust; this dust I strewed in the aperture of my window, making use of the loosened night-table to stand upon. I tied splinters from my bedstead together, with the ravelled yarn of an old stocking, and to this affixed a tuft of my hair. I worked a large hole under the middle grating, which could not be seen when standing on

the

the ground, and through this I
pushed my duft with the tool I had
prepared to the outer window, then,
waiting till the wind fhould happen
to rife, during the night I brufhed
it away, it was blown off, and no
appearance remained·on the outfide.
By this fingle expedient I rid myfelf
of, at leaft, three hundred weight of
earth, and thus made room to continue my labours: yet, this being
ftill infufficient, I had recourfe to
another artifice, which was, to knead
up the earth in the form of faufages,
to refemble the human fæces: thefe
I dried, and, when the prifoner came
to clean my dungeon, haftily toffed
them into the night-table, and thus
difencumbered myfelf of a pound or
two more of earth each week. I,
further, made little balls, and, when
the centinel was walking, blew
them, through a paper tube, out of

                    the

the window. Into the empty fpace
I put my mortar and ftones, and
worked on fuccefsfully.

I cannot, however, defcribe my
difficulties, after having penetrated
about two feet into the hewn ftone.
My tools were the irons I had dug
out, which faftened my bedftead and
night-table. A compaffionate foldier, alfo, gave me an old iron ram-
rod, and a foldier's fheath-knife,
which did me excellent fervice, more
efpecially, the latter, as I fhall, prefently, more fully fhew. With thefe,
too, I cut fplinters from my bedftead,
which aided me to pick the mortar
from the interftices of the ftone:
yet the labour of penetrating through
this feven-feet wall was incredible:
the building was ancient, and the
mortar, occafionally, quite petrified,
fo that the whole ftone was obliged to
be reduced to duft. After continu-
ing

ing my work, unremittingly, for fix months, I, at length, approached the accomplifhment of my hopes, as I knew, by coming to the facing of brick, which, now, was only between me and the adjoining cafemate.

Meantime I found opportunity to fpeak to fome of the centinels, among whom was an old grenadier called Gefhardt, whom I here name, becaufe he difplayed qualities of the greateft, and moft noble, kind. From him I learned the precife fituation of my prifon, and every circumftance that might beft conduce to my efcape.

Nothing was wanting but money to buy a boat, and, croffing the Elbe with Gefhardt, to take refuge in Saxony. By Gefhardt's means I became acquainted with a kindhearted girl, a Jewefs, and a native

of

of Deſſau, Eſther Heymannin by name, and whoſe father had been ten years in priſon. This good, compaſſionate maiden, whom I had never ſeen, won over two other grenadiers, who gave her an opportunity of ſpeaking to me every time they ſtood centinel. By tying my ſplinters together, I made a ſtick long enough to reach beyond the paliſadoes that were before my window, and thus obtained paper, another knife, and a file.

I, now, wrote to my ſiſter, the wife of the before-mentioned only ſon of General Waldow, deſcribed my ſituation, and intreated her to remit three hundred rix-dollars to the Jewefs, hoping, by this means, I might eſcape from my priſon. I wrote another affecting letter to Count Puebla, the Auſtrian ambaſſador, at Berlin, in which was incloſed

a draft,

a draft, for a thoufand florins, on my effects at Vienna, defiring him to remit thefe to the Jewefs, having promifed her that fum, as a reward for her fidelity. She was to bring the three hundred rix-dollars my fifter fhould fend to me, and take meafures, with the grenadiers, to facilitate my flight, which nothing feemed able to prevent, I having the power either to break into the cafe-mate, or, aided by the grenadiers and the Jewefs, to cut the locks from the doors, and, that way, efcape from my dungeon. The letters were open, I being obliged to roll them round the ftick to convey them to Efther.

The faithful girl ftraightway proceeded to Berlin, where fhe arrived fafe, and, immediately, fpoke to Count Puebla. The Count gave her the kindeft reception, received

the

the letter, with the letter of exchange, and bade her go and fpeak
to Weingarten, the fecretary of the
embaffy, and act entirely as he fhould
direct. She was received by Weingarten in the moft friendly manner,
who, by his queftions, drew from her
the whole fecret, and our intended
plan of flight, aided by the two grenadiers, and, alfo, that fhe had a letter for my fifter, which fhe muft carry to Hammer, near Cuftrin. He
afked to fee this letter, read it, told
her to proceed on her journey, gave
her two ducats to bear her expences,
ordered her to come to him on her
return, faid that, during this interval, he would endeavour to obtain
her the thoufand florins for my
draft, and would then give her further inftructions.

Efther, cheerfully, departed for
Hammer, where my fifter, then a
widow,

widow, and no longer, as in 1746, in dread of her hufband, joyful to hear I was ftill living, immediately gave her the three hundred rix-dollars, exhorting her to exert every poffible means to obtain my deliverance. Efther haftened back, with the letter from my fifter to me, to Berlin, and told all that had paffed to Weingarten, who read the letter, and enquired the names of the two grenadiers. He told her the thoufand florins, from Vienna, were not yet come, but gave her twelve ducats, bade her haften back to Magdeburg, to carry me all this good news, and then to return to Berlin, where he would pay her the thoufand florins. Efther came to Magdeburg, went, immediately, to the citadel, and, moft luckily, met the wife of one of the grenadiers, who told her that her hufband and his

com-

comrade had been taken, and put in irons the day before. Efther had quicknefs of perception, and fufpected we had been betrayed: fhe, therefore, inftantly again began her travels, and happily came fafe to Deffau.

Here I muft interrupt my narrative, that I may explain this infernal enigma to my readers, an account of which I received, after I had obtained my freedom, and ftill poffefs, in the hand-writing of this Jewefs. Wein-garten, as was afterwards difcovered, was a traitor, and too much trufted by Count Puebla, he being a fpy in the pay of Pruffia, and who had revealed to the court of Berlin, not only the fecrets of the Imperial embaffy, but alfo the whole plan of the projected war. For this reafon, he afterward, when war broke out, remained at Berlin, in the Pruffian fervice.

vice. His reason for betraying me was that he might secure the thousand florins, which I had drawn for on Vienna; for the receipt of the 24th of May, 1755, attests that the sum was paid, by the administrators of my effects, to Count Puebla, and has since been brought to account; nor can I believe that Weingarten did not appropriate this sum to himself, since I cannot be persuaded the ambassador would commit such an action, although the receipt is in his hand-writing, as may easily be demonstrated, it being now in my possession. Thus did Weingarten, that he might detain a thousand florins, with impunity, bring new evils upon me, and upon my sister, which occasioned her premature death; caused one grenadier to run the gauntlet, three successive days, and another to be hung.

Esther

Efther alone efcaped, and, fince, gave me an elucidation of the whole affair. The report at Magdeburg was that a Jewefs had obtained money from my fifter, and bribed two grenadiers, and that one of thefe had trufted, and been betrayed by his comrade. Indeed, what other ftory could be told at Magdeburg, or how could it be known I had been betrayed to the Pruffian miniftry by the Imperial fecretary? The truth, however, is as I have ftated; my account book exifts, and the Jewefs is ftill alive.

Her poor imprifoned father was punifhed with more than a hundred blows, to make him declare whether his daughter had intrufted him with the plot, or if he knew whither fhe was fled, and miferably died in fetters. Such was the mif-chief occafioned by a rafcal! And who

might

might be blamed but the imprudent Count Puebla?

In the year 1766, the Jewefs demanded of me a thoufand florins; and I wrote to Count Puebla, that, having his receipt for the fum, which never had been repaid, I begged it might be reftored. He received my agent with rudenefs, returned no anfwer, and feemed to trouble himfelf little concerning my lofs. Whether the heirs of the count be, or be not, indebted to me thefe thoufand florins, and the intereft, I leave the world to determine. Thrice have I been betrayed at Vienna, and fold to Berlin, like Jofeph to the Egyptians. My hiftory proves the origin of my misfortunes was the perfuafion that refidents, envoys, and ambaffadors, muft be men of known worth and honefty, and not the vileft of rafcals and mifcreants. But, alas!

the

the effects and money they have robbed me of have never been restored; and, for the miseries they have brought upon me, they could not be recompensed by the wealth of any or all the monarchs on earth. Estates they may, but truth they cannot, confiscate; and of the villainy of Abramson and Weingarten, I have documents and proofs that no court of justice could disannul. — Stop, reader, if thou hast a heart, and in that heart compassion ! Stop, and imagine what my sensations are, while I remember, and recount, a part only of the injustice that has been done me, a part only of the tyranny I have endured ! By this last act of treachery, of Weingarten, was I held in chains, the most horrible, for nine succeeding years ! By him was an innocent man brought to the gallows! By him, too, my sister, my beloved,

my

my unfortunate fifter, was obliged to build a dungeon for me, at her own expence! Befide being amerced in a fine, the extent of which I never could learn. Her goods were plundered, her eftates made a defert, her children fell into extreme poverty, and fhe, herfelf, expired in her thirty-third year, the victim of cruelty, perfecution, her brother's misfortunes, and the treachery of the Imperial embaffy!

Bleffed fhade of a beloved fifter!— The facrifice of my adverfe and dreadful fate! Thee could I never avenge! Thee could the blood of Weingarten never appeafe! No afylum, however facred, fhould have fecured him, had he not fought that laft of afylums for human wickednefs and human woes, the grave! To thee do I dedicate thefe few pages, a tribute of thankfulnefs; and, if future re-

wards

wards there are, may the brighteft of thefe rewards be thine! For us, nor for ours, may rewards be expected from monarchs who in apathy have beheld our mortal fufferings. Reft, noble foul, murdered, though thou wert, by the enemies of thy brother! Again my blood boils, again the tears roll down my cheeks, when I remember thee, thy fufferings in my caufe, and thy untimely end! I knew it not—I fought to thank thee — I found thee in the grave—I would have made retribution to thy children, but unjuft, ironhearted princes had deprived me of the power.—Can the virtuous heart conceive affliction more cruel? My own ills I would have endured with magnanimity; but thine are wrongs I have neither the power to forget nor heal.

Enough

(i) Enough of this. ——

The worthy Emperor, Francis I. fhed tears, when I afterward had the honour of relating to him, in perfon, my paft miferies; I beheld them flow, and gratitude threw me at his feet. His emotion was fo great, he tore himfelf away! I left the palace with all that enthufiafm of foul which fuch a fcene muft infpire.

He, probably, would have done more than pitied me, but his death foon followed. I relate this incident to convince pofterity Francis I. poffeffed a heart worthy an emperor, worthy of a man. In the knowledge I have had of monarchs, he ftands alone. Frederic and Therefa both died without doing me juftice; I am now too old, too proud, have too much apathy, to expect it from their fucceffors. Petition I will not, knowing my rights; and juſtice from courts of law, however evident my claims, were, in theſe courts, vain indeed to expeȼt. — Lawyers and advocates I know but too well, and an army to ſupport my rights I have not.

What heart that can feel but will pardon me theſe digreſſions! At the exaȼt and ſimple recital of faȼts like theſe, the whole man muſt be rouſed, and the philoſopher him-ſelf ſhudder.

Once more :—I heard nothing of what had happened for ſome days; at length, however, it was the honeſt Gefhardt's turn to mount guard; but, the poſts being doubled, and two additional grenadiers placed before my door, explanation was exceed-ingly difficult. He, however, in ſpite of precaution, found means to inform me what had happened to his two unfortunate comrades.

The

The King came to a review at Magdeburg, when he vifited the Star-Fort, and commanded a new cell to be immediately made, prefcribing himfelf the kind of irons by which I was to be fecured. The honeft Gefhardt heard the officer fay this cell was meant for me; gave me notice of it, but affured me it could not be ready in lefs than a month. I, therefore, determined, as foon as poffible, to complete my breach in the wall, and efcape, without the aid of any one. The thing was poffible; for I had twifted the hair of my matrafs into a rope, which I meant to tie to a cannon, and defcend the rampart, after which I might fwim acrofs the Elbe, gain the Saxon frontiers, and thus fafely efcape.

On the 26th of May I had determined to break into the next cafe-

C 2

mate;

mate; but, when I came to work at the bricks, I found them so hard, and strongly cemented, that I was obliged to defer the labour to the following day. I left off, weary and spent, at day-break, and, should any one enter my dungeon, they must infallibly discover the breach. How dreadful is the destiny by which, through life, I have been persecuted, and which has continually plunged me headlong into calamity, when I imagined happiness was at hand!

The 27th of May was a cruel day in the history of my life. My cell, in the Star-Fort, had been finished sooner than Gefhardt had supposed; and, at night, when I was preparing to fly, I heard a carriage stop before my prison. Oh, God! what was my terror, what were the horrors of this moment of despair! The locks and bolts resounded, the doors

flew

flew open, and the laſt of my poor remaining reſources was to conceal my knife. The town-major, the major of the day, and a captain entered; I ſaw them by the light of their two lanterns. The only words they ſpoke were, " dreſs yourſelf," which was immediately done. I ſtill wore the uniform of the regiment of Cordova. Irons were given me, which I was obliged myſelf to faſten on my wriſts and ancles: the town-major tied a bandage over my eyes, and, taking me under the arm, they thus conducted me to the carriage. It was neceſſary to paſs through the city to arrive at the Star-Fort: all was ſilent, except the noiſe of the eſcort; but, when we entered Magdeburg, I heard the people running, who were crowding together, to obtain a ſight of me. Their curioſity was raiſed, by the report that

I was

I was going to be beheaded. That I was executed, on this occasion, in the Star-Fort, after having been conducted blind-fold through the city, has since been both affirmed and written, and the officers had then orders to propagate this error, that the world might remain in utter ignorance concerning me. I, indeed, knew otherwife, though I affected not to have this knowledge; and, as I was not gagged, I behaved as if I expected death; — reproached my conductors in language that even made them fhudder, and painted their king in his true colours, as one who, unheard, had condemned an innocent fubject by a defpotic exertion of power.

My fortitude was admired, at the moment when it was fuppofed I thought myfelf leading to execution. No one replied, but their fighs inti-
mated

mated their compaſſion: certain it is, few Pruſſians willingly execute ſuch commands. The carriage, at length, ſtopped, and I was brought into my new cell. The bandage was taken from my eyes. The dungeon was lighted by a few torches. God of heaven! — what were my feelings, when I beheld the whole floor covered with chains, a fire-pan, and two grim men ſtanding with their ſmith-hammers!

* * * * * * * * * *

To work went theſe engines of deſpotiſm!—Enormous chains were fixed to my ancle at one end, and at the other to a ring which was incorporated in the wall. This ring was three feet from the ground, and only allowed me to move about two or three feet to the right and left. They next rivetted another huge iron ring, of a hand's breadth, round

C 4

my

my naked body, to which hung a chain, fixed into an iron bar, as thick as a man's arm. This bar was two feet in length, and at each end of it was a handcuff, as reprefented in the plate. The iron collar round my neck was not added till the year 1756.

* * * * * * * *

No foul bade me good-night.—All retired in dreadful filence;—and I heard the horrible grating of four doors, that were fucceffively locked and bolted upon me!

Thus does man act by his fellow, knowing him to be innocent, having received the commands of another man fo to act.

Oh God! thou, alone, knoweft how my heart, void as it was of guilt, beat at this moment. There fat I, deftitute, alone, in thick darknefs, upon the bare earth, with a

weight

weight of fetters infupportable to nature, thanking thee that thefe cruel men had not difcovered my knife, by which my miferies might yet find an end. Death is a laft, certain refuge, that can, indeed, bid defiance to the rage of tyranny. What fhall I fay? How fhall I make the reader feel as I then felt? How defcribe my defpondency, and yet account for that latent impulfe that withheld my hand on this fatal, this miferable night?

This mifery, I forefaw, was not of fhort duration: I had heard of the wars that were lately broken out between Auftria and Pruffia. Patiently to wait their termination, amid fufferings and wretchednefs, fuch as mine, appeared impoffible; and freedom even then was doubtful. Sad experience had I had of Vienna, and well I knew thofe, who had de-

spoiled

fpoiled me of my property, moft anx-
ioufly would endeavour to prevent
my return.—Such were my meditations ! Such my night thoughts !
Day at length returned—But where
was its fplendor ? Fled—I beheld
it not—Yet was its glimmering obfcurity fufficient to fhew me what
was my dungeon.

In breadth it was about eight feet;
in length, ten.   Near me once more
ftood a night table; in a corner was
a feat, four bricks broad, on which I
might fit, and recline againft the
wall.   Oppofite the ring to which.
I was faftened, the light was admitted through a femicircular aperture,
one foot high, and two in diameter.
This aperture afcended to the centre
of the wall, which was fix feet thick,
and at this central part was a clofe
iron grating, from which, outward,
the aperture defcended, and its two

extre-

extremities were again fecured by
ftrong iron bars. My dungeon was
built in the ditch of the fortification,
and the aperture, by which the light
entered, was fo covered by the wall
of the rampart that, inftead of finding immediate paffage, the light
only gained admiffion by reflection.
This, confidering the fmallnefs of
the aperture, and the impediments
of grating and iron bars, muft needs
make the obfcurity great, yet my
eyes, in time, became fo accuftomed
to this glimmering that I could fee
a moufe run. In winter, however,
when the fun did not fhine into the
ditch, it was eternal night with me.
Between the bars and the grating
was a glafs window, with a fmall
central cafement, which might be
opened to admit air. My night-
table was daily removed, and befide
me ftood a jug of water. The

C 6 name

name of TRENCK was built in the wall, in red brick, and under my feet was a tombſtone, with the name of TRENCK alſo cut on it, and carved with a death's head. The doors to my dungeon were double, of oak, two inches thick: without theſe was an open ſpace or front cell, in which was a window, and this ſpace was, likewiſe, ſhut in by double doors. The ditch, in which this dreadful den was built, was incloſed on both ſides by paliſadoes, twelve feet high, the key of the door of which was entruſted to the officer of the guard, it being the King's intention to prevent all poſſibility of ſpeech or communication with the centinels, The only motion I had the power to make was that of jumping upward, or ſwinging my arms, to procure myſelf warmth. When more accuſtomed to theſe fetters, I was, likewiſe,

capa-

capable of moving from side to side, about four feet, but this pained my shin bones.

The cell had been finished with lime and plaister but eleven days, and every body supposed it would be impossible I should exist in these damps above a fortnight. I remained six months, continually immersed in water, that trickled upon me from the thick arches under which I was; and I can safely affirm that, for the first three months, I was never dry; yet did I continue in health. I was visited daily, at noon, after relieving guard, and the doors were then obliged to be left open for some minutes, otherwise the dampness of the air put out their candles.

This was my situation, and here I sat, destitute of friend, helplessly wretched, preyed on by all the tor-

ture

ture of thought, that continually suggested the most gloomy, the most dreadful of images. My heart was not yet wholly turned to stone, my fortitude was sunken to despondency; my dungeon was the very cave of despair; yet was my arm restrained, yet was this excess of misery endured.

How, then, may hope be wholly eradicated from the heart of man! My fortitude, after some time, began to revive; I glowed with the desire of convincing the world I was capable of suffering what man had never suffered before, perhaps of, at last, emerging from this load of wretchednefs, triumphant over my enemies. So long, and ardently, did my fancy dwell on this picture that my mind, at length, acquired a heroism, which Socrates himself certainly never poffessed. Age had

benumbed

benumbed his fenfe of pleafure, and he drank the poifonous draught, with cool indifference; I was young, inured to high hopes, yet now beholding deliverance impoffible, or at an immenfe, a dreadful diftance. Such, too, were the fufferings of foul, and body, I could not hope they might be fupported and live.

About noon my den was opened. Sorrow and compaffion were painted on the countenances of my keepers. No one fpoke. No one had me good-morrow. Dreadful, indeed, was their arrival, for, unaccuftomed to the monftrous bolts and bars, they were kept refounding for a full half hour, before fuch foul-chilling, fuch hope-murdering, im-pediments were removed. It was the voice of tyranny that thundered!

My night-table was taken out, a camp-bed, matrafs, and blankets, were

were brought me; a jug of water
fat down, and, befide it, an ammunition loaf of fix pounds weight.
" That you no more may complain
" of hunger," faid the town-major,
" you fhall have as much bread
" as you can eat." The door was
fhut, and I again left to my thoughts.

What a ftrange thing is that called
happinefs! How fhall I exprefs my
extreme joy, when, after eleven
months of intolerable hunger, I was
again indulged with a full feaft of
coarfe ammunition bread? The
fond lover never rufhed more eagerly
to the arms of his expecting bride;
the famifhed tiger more ravenoufly
on his prey, than I upon this loaf:
I eat, refted, furveyed the precious
morfel, eat again, and, abfolutely,
fhed tears of pleafure——Breaking
bit after bit, I had, by evening,
devoured all my loaf.

Oh

Oh Nature! what delight haſt thou combined with the gratification of thy wants! Remember this, ye who gorge, ye who rack invention to excite appetite, and which yet you cannot procure; remember how ſimple are the means that will give a cruſt of mouldy bread a flavour more exquiſite than all the ſpices of the Eaſt, or all the profuſion of land or ſea; remember this, grow hungry, and indulge your ſenſuality.

Alas! my enjoyment was of ſhort duration. I ſoon found that exceſs is followed by pain and repentance. My faſting had weakened digeſtion, and rendered it inactive. My body ſwelled, my water-jug was emptied, cramps, cholics, and, at length, inordinate thirſt racked me all the night. I began to pour curſes on thoſe who ſeemed to refine

on

on torture, and, after starving me so long, to invite me to gluttony. Could I not have reclined on my bed, I should, indeed, have been driven, this night, to desperation: yet, even this was but a partial relief, for, not yet accuftomed to my enormous fetters, I could not extend myfelf in them in the fame manner I was afterward taught to do by habit. I dragged them, however, fo together as to enable me to fit down on the bare matrafs. This, of all my nights of fuffering, ftands foremoft. When they opened my dungeon, next day, they found me in a truly pitiable fituation, wondered at my appetite, brought me another loaf; I refufed to accept it, believing I never more fhould have occafion for bread : they, however, left me one, gave me water, fhrugged up their fhoulders, wifhed me

farewell,

farewell, as, according to all appearance, they never expected to find
me alive, and shut all the doors,
without asking whether I wished, or
needed, farther assistance.

Three days had passed before I
could again eat a morsel of bread,
and my mind, brave in health, now,
in a sick body, became pusillani-
mous, so that I determined on death.
The irons, every where round my
body, and their weight, were insupportable; nor could I imagine it
was possible I should habituate myself to them, or endure them long
enough to expect deliverance. Peace
was a very distant prospect. The
King had commanded that such a
prison should be built as should ex-
clude all necessity of a centinel, in
order that I might not converse with
and seduce them from what is called
their duty; and, in the first days of
despair,

defpair, deliverance appeared impoſſible; and the fetters, the war, the pain
I felt, the place, the length of time,
each circumſtance ſeemed equally
impoſſible to ſupport. A thouſand reaſons convinced me it was
neceſſary to end my ſufferings. I
ſhall not enter into theological diſ-
putes: let thoſe who blame me
imagine themſelves in my ſituation;
or, rather, let them firſt actually
endure my miſeries, and, then, let
them reaſon. I had, often, braved
death in proſperity, and, at this
moment, it ſeemed a bleſſing.

Full of theſe meditations, every
minute's patience appeared abſur-
dity, and reſolution meanneſs of
ſoul, yet I wiſhed my mind ſhould
be ſatisfied that reaſon, and not
raſhneſs, had induced the act. I,
therefore, determined, that I might
examine the queſtion coolly, to
wait

wait a week longer, and die on the fourth of July. In the meantime I revolved in my mind what possible means there were of escape, not fearing, naked and chained, to rush and expire on the bayonets of my enemies.

The next day I observed, as the four doors were opened, that they were only of wood, therefore, questioned whether I might not even cut off the locks with the knife that I had so fortunately concealed; and, should this and every other means fail, then would be the time to die. I, likewise, determined to make an attempt even to free myself of my chains. I, happily, forced my right hand through the hand-cuff, though the blood trickled from my nails. My attempts on the left were long ineffectual: but, by rubbing with a brick, which I got from my feat, on the rivet

that

that had been negligently clofed, I effected this alfo.

The chain was faftened to the rim round my body, by a hook, one end of which was not inferted in the rim, therefore, by fetting my foot againft the wall, I had ftrength enough fo far to bend this hook back, and open it, as to force out the link of the chain. The remaining difficulty was the chain that attached my foot to the wall: the links of this chain I took, doubled, twifted, and wrenched, till, at length, nature having beftowed on me great ftrength, I made a defperate effort, fprang forcibly up, and two links, at once, flew off.

Fortunate, indeed, did I think my-felf; I haftened to the door, groped in the dark to find the clinchings of the nails by which the lock was faftened, and difcovered no very large piece

of

of wood need be cut. Immediately I went to work with my knife, and cut through the oak door, to find its thickness, which proved to be only one inch, therefore, was it possible to open all the four doors in four and twenty hours.

Again hope revived in my heart. To prevent detection I haftened to put on my chains; but, oh God! what difficulties had I to furmount! After much groping about, I, at length, found the link that had flown off; this I hid. It had been my good fortune, hitherto, to efcape examination, as the possibility of ridding myfelf of fuch chains was in no wife fufpected. The feparated links I tied together with my hair ribbon; but, when I again endeavoured to force my hand into the ring, it was fo fwelled that every effort was fruitlefs. The whole

night

night was employed upon the rivet, but all labour was in vain.

Noon was the hour of vifitation, and neceffity and danger again obliged me to attempt forcing my hand in, which, at length, after excruciating torture, I' effected. My vifitors came, and every thing had the appearance of order. I found it, however, impoffible to force out my right hand while it continued fwelled.

I, therefore, remained quiet till the day fixed, and, on the determined fourth of July, immediately as my vifitors had clofed the doors upon me, I difincumbered myfelf of my irons, took my knife, and began my Herculean labour on the door. The firft of the double doors that opened inwards was conquered in lefs than an hour; the other was a very different tafk. The lock was foon cut round, but it opened outwards; there were, therefore, no other means left, but to cut the whole door away above the bar.

This inceffant and incredible labour made poffible, though it was the more difficult, as every thing was to be done by feeling, I being totally in the dark; the fweat dropt, or, rather, flowed from my body; my fingers were clotted with my own blood, and my lacerated hands were one continued wound.

Day-light appeared, I clambered over the door that was half cut away, and got up to the window in the fpace or cell that was between the double doors, as before defcribed. Here I faw my dungeon was in the ditch of the firft rampart: before me I beheld the road from the rampart, the guard but fifty paces diftant, and the high palifadoes that were in the ditch, and muſt be ſcaled before I could reach the rampart. Hope grew ſtronger; my efforts were redoubled. The firſt of the next double doors was attacked, which, likewiſe, opened inward, and was ſoon conquered. The ſun ſet before I had ended this, and the fourth was to be cut away, as the ſecond had been. My ſtrength failed; both my hands were raw: I reſted a while, began again, and had made a cut of a foot long, when my knife ſnapt, and the broken blade dropt to the ground.

* * * * * * * * * *

God of omnipotence! what was I at this moment! Was there, God of mercies! was there ever creature of thine more juſtified than I in deſpair?——The moon ſhone clear; I caſt a wild and diſtracted look up to Heaven, fell on my knees, and,

in

in the agony of my foul, fought
comfort; but no comfort could be
found, nor Religion nor Philofophy
had any to give.——I curfed not
Providence, I feared not annihilation, I dared not Almighty vengeance; God the creator was the
difpofer of my fate; and, if he heap-
·ed afflictions upon me he had not
given me ftrength to fupport, his juftice would not, therefore, punifh me.
To him, the Judge of the quick and
dead, I committed my foul, feized the
broken knife, gafhed through the veins
of my left arm and foot, fat myfelf
tranquilly down, and faw the blood
flow. Nature, overpowered, fainted,
and I know not how long I remained flumbering in this ftate——
Suddenly I heard my own name,
awoke, and again heard the words
Baron Trenck! My anfwer was,
who calls?—And who indeed was

 it—

it—who but my honeſt grenadier Gefhardt—my former faithful friend in the citadel.——The good, the kind, fellow had got upon the rampart, that he might comfort me.

"How do you do?" ſaid Gefhardt——"Weltering in my blood," anſwered I; "to-morrow you will find me dead."——"Why ſhould you die?" replied he. "It is much "eaſier for you to eſcape here than "from the citadel. Here is no "centinel, and I ſhall ſoon find "means to provide you with tools: "if you can only break out, leave "the reſt to me. As often as I am "on guard I will ſeek opportunity "to ſpeak to you. In the whole "Star-Fort there are but two cen- "tinels; the one at the entrance, "and the other at the guard-houſe. "——Do not deſpair, God will ſuc- "cour you; truſt to me."——The

good

good man's kindnefs and difcourfe
revived my hopes: I faw the poffi-
bility of an efcape. A fecret joy
diffufed itfelf through my foul——
I, immediately, tore my fhirt, bound
up my wounds, and waited the approach of day; and the fun, foon
after, fhone through the window,
to me, with unaccuftomed bright-
nefs.

Let the reader judge how far it
was chance, how far the effect of
divine providence, that in this dreadful hour my heart again received
hope. Who was it fent the honeft
Gefhardt, at fuch a moment, to my
prifon? For, had it not been for him,
I had, certainly, when I awoke from
my flumbers, cut more effectually
through my arteries.

Till noon I had time to confider
what might farther be done: yet,
what could be done, what expected,

but

but that I should now be much more cruelly treated, and even more insupportably ironed than before; finding, as they must, the doors cut through, and my fetters shaken off?

After mature confideration, I, therefore, made the following refolution, which fucceeded happily, and even beyond my hopes. Before I proceed, however, I will fpeak a few words concerning my then fituation. It is impoffible to defcribe how much I was exhaufted. The prifon fwam with blood, and, certainly, but little was left in my body. With painful wounds, fwelled and torn hands, I there ftood, fhirtlefs, felt an inclination to fleep almoft irrefiftible, and fcarcely had ftrength to keep my legs, yet was I obliged to roufe myfelf, that I might execute my plan.

With the bar that feparated my

hands

hands I loofened the bricks of my feat, which, being newly laid, was eafily done, and heaped them up in the middle of my prifon. The inner door was quite open, and with my chains I fo barricadoed the upper half of the fecond as to prevent any one climbing over it. When noon came, and the firft of the doors was unlocked, all were aftonifhed to find the fecond open. There I ftood, a defperate man, befmeared with blood, the picture of horror, with a brick in one hand, and in the other my broken knife, crying, as they approached, " Keep " off, Mr. Major, keep off!———— " Tell the Governor I will live no " longer in chains, and that here I " ftand, if fo he pleafes, to be fhot; " for fo only will I be conquered. " Here no man fhall enter—I will " deftroy all that approach; here are

" my

" my weapons, here will I die in de-
" fpite of tyranny."   The major was
terrified, wanted refolution, and made
his report to the governor. I, meantime, fat down on my bricks, to wait
what might happen: my fecret intent, however, was not fo defperate
as it appeared. I fought only to
obtain a favourable capitulation.

The governor, General Borck,
prefently, came, attended by the
town-major, and fome officers, and
entered the outward cell, but fprung
back the moment he beheld a figure
like me, ftanding with a brick and
up-lifted arm. I repeated what I
had told the major, and he, immediately, ordered fix grenadiers to
force the door. The front cell was
fcarcely fix feet broad, fo that no
more than two at a time could attack my intrenchment, and, when
they faw my threatening bricks
ready

ready to defcend, they leaped, terrified, back. A fhort paufe enfued,
and the old town-major, with the
chaplain, advanced toward the door
to footh me: the converfation continued fome time; whofe reafons
were moft fatisfactory, and whofe
caufe was the moft juft, I leave to
the reader. The governor grew
angry, and ordered a frefh attack.
The firft grenadier was knocked
down, and the reft ran back to avoid
my miffiles.

The town-major, again, began
a parley. " For God's fake, my dear
" Trenck," faid he, " in what have I
" injured you, that you endeavour
" to effect my ruin? I muft anfwer
" for your having, through my neg-
" ligence, concealed a knife. Be
" perfuaded, I intreat you. Be ap-
" peafed. You are not without
" hope, nor without friends."—My

 anfwer

anfwer was,—" But will you not
" load me with ·heavier irons than
" before ?"

He went out, fpoke with the governor, and gave me his word of honour that the affair fhould be no
farther noticed, and that every thing
fhould be exactly reinftated as formerly.

Here ended the capitulation, and
my wretched citadel was taken.
The condition I was in was viewed
with pity ; my wounds were examined, a furgeon fent to drefs them,
another fhirt was given me, and the
bricks, clotted with blood, removed.
I, mean time, lay half dead on my
matrafs: my thirft was exceffive, the
furgeon ordered me fome wine; two
centinels were ftationed in the front
cell, and I was thus left, four days,
in peace, unironed. Broth, alfo, was
given me daily, and how delicious

                             this

this was to tafte, how much it revived and ftrengthened me, is wholly
impoffible to defcribe.   Two days
I lay in a flumbering kind of trance,
forced, by unquenchable thirft, to
drink whenever I awoke.   My feet
and hands were fwelled; the pains
in my back, and limbs, were exceffive.

On the fifth day, the doors were
ready; the inner was entirely plated
with iron, and I was fettered as before: perhaps, they found further
cruelty unneceffary.   The principal
chain, however, which faftened me
to the wall, like that I had before
broken, was thicker than the firft.
Except this, the capitulation was
ftrictly kept. They deeply regretted
that, without the King's exprefs commands, they could not lighten my
afflictions, wifhed me fortitude and
patience, and barred up my doors, .

D 6   It

It is neceffary I fhould here defcribe my drefs. My hands being
fixed and kept afunder, by an iron
bar, and my feet chained to the wall,
I could neither put on fhirt or ftock-
ings in the ufual mode; the fhirt
was, therefore, tied, as reprefented in
the plate, and changed once a fortnight; the coarfe ammunition ftock-
ings were buttoned on the fides; a
blue garment, of foldier's cloth, was
likewife tied round me, and I had
a pair of flippers for my feet. The
fhirt was of the army linen; and
when I contemplated myfelf in this
drefs of a malefactor, chained thus
to the wall, in fuch a dungeon,
vainly imploring mercy or juftice,
my confcience void of reproach,
my heart of guilt; when I reflected
on my former fplendor in Berlin and
Mofcow, and compared it with this
fad, this dreadful reverfe of deftiny,

I was

I was funk in grief, or roufed to indignation, that might have hurried the greateſt hero, or philoſopher, to madneſs or deſpair. I felt what can only be imagined by him who has ſuffered like me, after having, like me, flouriſhed, if ſuch can be found.

Pride, the juſtneſs of my cauſe, the unbounded confidence I had in my own reſolution, and the labours of an inventive head and iron body, theſe, only, could have preſerved my life. Theſe bodily labours, theſe continued inventions, and projected plans, to obtain my freedom, preſerved my health. Who would ſuppoſe that a man, fettered, as I was, could find means of exerciſing himſelf? By ſwinging my arms, acting with the upper part of my body, and leaping upward, I frequently put myſelf in a ſtrong perſpiration.

After

After thus wearying myfelf, I flept foundly, and often thought how many generals, obliged to fupport all the inclemencies of weather, and all the dangers of the field ; how many of thofe who had plunged me into this den of mifery, would have been moft glad, could they, like me, have flept with a quiet confcience. Often did I reflect how much happier I was than thofe tortured on the bed of ficknefs, by gout, ftone, and other difeafes, terrible to man. How much happier was I in innocence, than the malefactor doomed to fuffer the pangs of death, the ignominy of men, and the horrors of internal guilt !

In the following part of my hiftory it will appear I often had much money concealed under the ground, and in the walls of my den, yet, would I have given a hundred ducats

for

for a morfel of bread, it could not
have been procured. Money was
to me ufelefs. In this I refembled
the mifer, who hoards, yet lives in
wretchednefs, having no joy in gen-
tle acts of benevolence. As proudly
might I delight myfelf with my
hidden treafure, as fuch mifers, nay
more, for I was fecure from robbers.

Had faftidious pomp been my
pleafure, I might have imagined
myfelf fome old field-marfhal bed-
ridden, who hears two grenadier centinels at his door call, " Who goes
" there ?" My honour, indeed, was
ftill greater, for, during my laft
year's imprifonment, my door was
guarded by no lefs than four. My
vanity, alfo, might have flattered
itfelf, I hence might conclude how
high was the value fet upon my
head, fince all this trouble was taken to hold me in fecurity. Certain

it

it is, that, in my chains, I thought more rationally, more nobly, reasoned more philosophically on man, his nature, his real, his imaginary wants; the effects of his ambition, his passions, and saw more distinctly his dream of earthly good, than those who had imprisoned me, or those who guarded. I was void of the fears that haunt the parasite, who servilely wears the fetters of a court, and daily trembles for the loss of what vice and cunning have acquired. Those who have usurped my Sclavonian estates, and feasted sumptuously from the service of plate I had been robbed of, never eat their dainties with so sweet an appetite as I my ammunition bread, nor did their high-flavoured wines flow so limpid as my cold water.

Thus the man, who thinks, being pure of heart, will find consolation,

when

when under the moſt dreadful of calamities, convinced, as he muſt be, that
thoſe apparently moſt happy are frequently leaſt, inſenſible as they are
of the pleaſures they might enjoy.
Evil never is ſo great as it appears.

" Sweet are the uſes of adverſity,
" Which, like the toad, ugly and venomous,
" Wears yet a precious jewel in its head.'
                        As you like it. *

Happy he, who, like me, having
ſuffered, can become an example to
his ſuffering brethren.

YOUTH, proſperous, and imagining proſperity eternal, read my hiſ-
tory attentively, though I ſhould be in
                                    my

* The Baron has quoted a poem written
and publiſhed by himſelf.

" Im uebel ſelbſt ſteckt noch ein preiß
" Wenn man ihn nur zu finden weiß."

The ſimilarity of the thought, which ſeems
borrowed from Shakeſpeare, juſtifies a quo-
tation ſo beautiful.   T.

my grave ! Read feelingly, and blefs my fleeping duft, if it has taught thee wifdom or fortitude !

FATHER, reading this, fay to thy. children, I, like them, in blooming youth, little prophefied of misfortune, which after fell thus heavy on me, and by which I am even ftill perfecuted ! Say that I had virtue,. ambition, was educated in noble principles ; that I laboured with all the zeal of enthufiaftic youth to become wifer, better, greater than other men ; that I was guilty of no crimes, was the friend of men, was no deceiver of man, or woman ; that I firft ferved my own country faithfully, and, after, every other in which I found bread ; that I was never,. during life, once intoxicated ; was no gamefter, no night rambler, no contemptible idler; that, yet, through envy and arbitrary power, I have

fallen

fallen to mifery, fuch as none but the worft of criminals ought to feel.

BROTHER, fly thofe countries where the lawgiver knows himfelf no law, where truth and virtue are punifhed as crimes : and, if fly you cannot, be it your endeavour to remain unknown, unnoticed, in fuch countries ; feek not favour or honourable employ, elfe will you become; when your merits are known, as I have been, the victim of flander and treachery ; the behefts of power will perfecute you, and innocence will not fhield you from the fhafts of wicked men who are envious, or who wifh to obtain the favour of princes, though by the worft of means.

SIRE, imagine not thou readeft a romance; my head is grey, like thine. Read, yet defpife not the world, though it has treated me thus un-
thank-

thankfully. Good men have I also found, who have befriended me in misfortune, and there, where leaſt I had claim, have I found them moſt. May my book aſſiſt thee in noble thoughts; mayſt thou die as tranquilly as I ſhall render up my ſoul to appear before the Judge of me and my perſecutors. Be death but thought a tranſition from motion to reſt. Few are the delights of this world, for him, who, like me, has learned to know it. Murmur not, deſpair not of Providence. Me, through ſtorms, it has brought to haven; through many griefs, to ſelf knowledge; and, through priſons, to philoſophy. He, only, can tranquilly deſcend to annihilation, who finds reaſon not to repent he has once exiſted. My rudder broke not, amid the rocks and quickſands, but my bark was wrecked upon the

ſtrand

ſtrand of knowledge. Yet, even on theſe clear ſhores, are impenetrable clouds. I have ſeen more diſtinctly than it is ſuppoſed men ought to ſee. Age will decay the faculties, and mental, like bodily ſight, muſt then decreaſe. I even grew weary of ſcience, and envied the blind-born, or thoſe who, till death, have been wilfully hood-winked. How often have I been aſked, " What didſt " thou ſee ? "—And, when I anſwered with ſincerity and truth, how often have I been derided as a liar, and been perſecuted, by thoſe who determined not to ſee themſelves, as an innovator, ſingular and raſh !

Sire, I farther ſay to thee, teach thy deſcendants to ſeek the golden mean, and ſay with Gellert—" The " boy Fritz needs nothing: his ſtu- " pidity will inſure his ſucceſs."— Examine our wealthy and titled lords,

lords, what their abilities are, and what their honours, then inquire how they were attained, and, if thou canſt, diſcover in what true happineſs conſiſts.

Once more to my priſon. The failure of my eſcape, and the recovery of life, from this ſtate of deſpair, led me to moralize deeper than I had ever done before; and, in this depth of thought, I found unexpected conſolation and fortitude, and a firm perſuaſion I yet ſhould accompliſh my deliverance.

Gefhardt, my honeſt grenadier, had infuſed freſh hope, and my mind now buſily began to meditate new plans. A centinel had been placed before my door, that I might be more narrowly watched, and the married men of the Pruſſian ſtates were appointed to this duty, who, as I ſhall hereafter ſhew, were more

eaſy

eafy to perfuade in aiding my flight, than foreign fugitives. The Pomeranian will liften, and is, by nature, kind, therefore, may eafily be moved, and induced to fuccour diftrefs.

I began to be more accuftomed to my irons, which I had before found fo infupportable; I could comb out my long hair, and could tie it at laft with one hand. My beard, which had fo long remained unfhaven, gave me a grim appearance, and I began to pluck it up by the roots. The pain, at firft, was confiderable, efpecially round the lips; but this, alfo, cuftom conquered, and I performed this operation in the following years, once in fix weeks, or two months; as the hair thus plucked up required that length of time before the nails could again get hold. Vermin did not moleft me; the dampnefs of my den was

inimi-

inimical to them. My limbs never fwelled, becaufe of the exercife I gave myfelf, as before defcribed. The greateft pain I found was in the continued unvivifying dimnefs in which I lived.

I had read much; had lived in, and feen much of, the world; vacuity·of thought, therefore, I was little troubled with; the former tranf-actions of my life, what had happen-ed, and the remembrance of the perfons I had known, I revolved fo often in my mind that they became as familiar and connected, as if the events had each been written in the order it occurred. Habit made this mental exercife fo perfect to me that I could compofe fpeeches, fables, odes, fatires, all which I repeated aloud, and had fo ftored my memory with them that I was enabled, after I had obtained my freedom, to com·

mit

mit to writing two volumes of thefe my prifon labours. Accuftomed to this exercife, days, that would other- wife have been days of mifery, ap- peared but as a moment. The fol- lowing narrative will fhew how much efteem, how many friends, thefe compofitions procured me, even in my dungeon, infomuch that I obtained light, paper, and, finally, freedom itfelf. For thefe have I to thank the induftrious acquirements of my youth, therefore, do I coun- fel all my readers fo to employ their time. Riches, honours, the favours of fortune, may be fhowered by mo- narchs upon the moft worthlefs; but monarchs can give and take, fay and unfay, raife and pull down. Monarchs, however, can neither give wifdom nor virtue. Arbitrary power itfelf, here, and before thefe, is foiled.

How wifely has Providence or-

    E   dained

dained that the endowments of induftry, learning, and fcience, given
by ourfelves, cannot be taken from
us; while, on the contrary, what
others beftow is a fantaftical dream,
from which any accident may awaken
us. The wrath of Frederic could
deftroy legions, and defeat armies;
but it could not take from me the
fenfe of honour, of innocence, and
their fweet concomitant, peace of
mind; could not deprive me of fortitude and magnanimity: I defied
his power, refted on the juftice of my
caufe, found in myfelf expedients
wherewith to oppofe him, was at
length crowned with conqueft, and
came forth, to the world, the martyr
of fuffering virtue.

Some of my oppreffors now rot
in difhonourable graves. Others,
alas! in Vienna, remain immured in
houfes of correction, as Krügel and
Zetto, or beg their bread, like Gravenitz

venitz and Doo. Nor are the wealthy poſſeſſors of my eſtates more fortunate, but look down with ſhame
whenever I and my children appear.
We ſtand erect, eſteemed, and honoured, while their injuſtice is ma-
nifeſt to the whole world.

Young man, be induſtrious, for,
without induſtry, can none of the
treaſures I have deſcribed be pur-
chaſed. Thy labour will reward
itſelf ; then, when aſſaulted by miſ-
fortune, or even miſery, learn of me,
and ſmile ; or, ſhouldeſt thou eſcape
ſuch trials, ſtill labour to acquire
wiſdom, that, in old age, thou may-
eſt find content and happineſs.

The years in my dungeon paſſed
away as days, thoſe moments excepted, when, thinking on the great
world, and the deeds of great men,
my ambition was rouſed : except
when, contemplating the vileneſs of
my chains, and the wretchedneſs of

E 2

my

my fituation, I laboured for liberty, and found my labours endlefs and ineffectual: except while I remembered the triumph of my enemies, and the fplendor in which thofe, by whom I had been plundered, lived. Then, indeed, did I experience intervals that approached madnefs, defpair, and horror: beholding myfelf deftitute of friend or protector, the Emprefs herfelf, for whofe fake I fuffered, deferting me; reflecting on paft times and paft profperity; remembering how the good and virtuous, from the cruel nature of my punifhment, muft be obliged to conclude me a wretch and a villain, and that all means of juftification were cut off; oh, God! How did my heart beat! With what violence! What would I not have undertaken, in thefe fuffering moments, to have put my enemies to fhame! Vengeance, and rage, then,

rofe

rofe rebellious againſt patience; long ſuffering philoſophy vaniſhed, and the poiſoned cup of Socrates would have been the nectar of the Gods.

Man, deprived of hope, is man deſtroyed. I found but little probability in all my plans and projects, yet did I truſt that ſome of them ſhould ſucceed, yet did I confide in them and my honeſt Gefhardt, and that I ſhould ſtill free myſelf from my chains.

The greateſt of all my incitements to patient endurance was love. I had left behind me, in Vienna, a lady, for whom the world ſtill was dear to me; her would I neither deſert nor afflict. To her and my ſiſter was my exiſtence ſtill neceſſary. For their ſakes, who had loſt and ſuffered ſo much for mine, would I preſerve my life; for them no difficulty, no ſuffering, was too great; yet them, alas! when long-deſired

liberty

liberty was reſtored, I found both in their graves. The joy, for which I had borne ſo much, was no more to be taſted.

About three weeks after my attempt to eſcape, the good Gefhardt firſt came to ſtand centinel over me; and the centinel they had ſo carefully ſet was, indeed, the only hope I could have of eſcape; for help muſt be had from without, or this was impoſſible.

The effort I had made had excited too much ſurpriſe and alarm for me to paſs without ſtrict examination, ſince, on the ninth day after I was confined, I had, in eighteen hours, ſo far broken through a priſon built purpoſely for myſelf, by a combination of ſo many projectors, and with ſuch extreme precaution, which priſon had univerſally been declared impenetrable.

Gefhardt ſcarcely had taken his
poſt

poft before we had free opportunity
of converfing together; for, when
I ftood, with one foot, on my bedftead, I could reach the aperture,
through which light was admitted.

Gefhardt defcribed the fituation
of my dungeon, and our firft plan
was to break through the foundation
which he had feen laid, and which he
affirmed to be only two feet deep.

Money was the firft thing neceffary. Gefhardt was relieved during
his guard, and returned, bringing
with him a fheet of paper rolled on
a wire, which he paffed through my
grating; after which a piece of fmall
wax-candle, fome burning amadoue
(a kind of tinder), a match, and a
pen. I now had light, pricked my
finger, and wrote, with my blood,
to my faithful friend, Captain Ruckhardt, at Vienna, defcribed my fituation in a few words, fent him an
acquittance for three thoufand flo-

rins

rins on my revenues, and requeſted he would diſpoſe of a thouſand florins to defray the expences of his journey to Gummern, only two miles from Magdeburg. Here he was, poſitively, to be on the 15th of Auguſt. About noon, on this ſame day, he was to walk, with a letter in his hand; a man was there to meet him, ſmoking a roll of tobacco, to whom he muſt remit the two thouſand florins, and return to Vienna.

I returned the written paper to Gefhardt by the ſame means it had been received, gave him my inſtructions, and he ſent his wife with it to Gummern, by whom it was ſafely put in the poſt.

My hopes daily roſe, and, as often as Gefhardt mounted guard, ſo often did we continue our projects. The 15th of Auguſt came, but it was ſome days before Gefhardt was again on guard; and oh! how did my

heart

heart palpitate when he came and
exclaimed, " All is right! we have
" fucceeded." He returned in the
evening, and we began to confider
by what means he could convey the
money to me. I could not, with
my hands chained to an iron bar,
reach to the aperture of the window
that admitted air; befide that it was,
too fmall. It was, therefore, agreed
that Gefhardt fhould, on the next
guard, perform the office of cleaning
my dungeon, and that he then fhould
convey the money to me in the
water-jug.

This, luckily, was done. How
great was my aftonifhment when,
inftead of one, I found two thoufand
florins! For I had permitted him to
referve half to himfelf, as a reward
for his fidelity. He, however, had
kept but five piftoles, which he perfifted was enough.

Worthy Gefhardt! This was the

 act

act of a Pomeranian grenadier! How rare are such examples! Be thy name and mine ever united. Live thou while the memory of me shall live. Never did my acquaintance with the great bring to my knowledge a soul so noble, so disinterested!

It is true, I, afterward, prevailed on him to accept the whole thousand; but we shall soon see he never had them, and that his foolish wife, three years after, suffered by their means; however, she suffered alone, for he soon marched to the field, and therefore was unpunished.

Having money to carry on my designs, I began to put my plan of burrowing under the foundation into execution. The first thing necessary was to free myself from my fetters. To accomplish this, Gefhardt supplied me with two small files, and, by the aid of these, this labour, though great, was effected.

The

The cap, or ftaple, of the foot-ring was made fo wide that I could draw it forward a quarter of an inch. I filed the iron which paffed through it on the infide, and the more I filed this away, the further I could draw the cap down, till at laft the whole infide iron, through which the chains paffed, was quite cut through; by this means I could flip off the ring, while the cap on the outfide conti-nued whole, and it was impoffible to difcover any cut, as only the outfide could be examined.. My hands, by continued efforts, I fo compreffed as to be able to draw them out of the hand-cuffs. I then filed the hinge,, and made a fcrew-driver of one of the foot-long flooring nails, by which I could take out the fcrews at plea-fure, fo that at the time of examina-tion no proofs could appear. The rim round my body was but a fmall.

impe-

impediment, except the cháin, which paffed from my hand-bar, and this I removed, by filing an aperture in one of the links, which, at the neceffary hour, I clofed with bread, rubbed over with rufty iron, firft drying it by the heat of my body; and would wager any fum that, without ftriking the chain, link by link, with a hammer, no one, not in the fecret, would have difcovered this fracture.

The window was never ftrictly examined; I, therefore, drew the two ftaples by which the iron bars were fixed to the wall, and which I daily replaced, carefully plaiftering them over. I procured wire from Gefhardt, and tried how well I could imitate the inner grating: finding I fucceeded tolerably, I cut the real grating totally away, and fubftituted an artificial one of my own fabricating, by which I obtained a free communication with the outfide,

addi-

additional frefh air, together with all neceffary implements, tinder and candles. That the light might not be feen, I hung the coverlid of my bed before the window, fo that I could work fearlefs and undetected.

Every thing prepared, I went to work. The floor of my dungeon was not of ftone, but oak planks, three inches thick; three beds of which were laid croffwife, and were faftened to each other by nails half an inch in diameter, and a foot long. Having worked round the head of a nail, I made ufe of the hole at the end of the bar, which feparated my hands, to draw it out, and this nail I fharpened upon my tomb-ftone into an excellent chiffel.

I now cut through the board more than an inch in width, that I might work downward, and, having drawn away a piece of board which was inferted two inches under the wall,

wall, I cut this fo as exactly to fit: the fmall crevice it occafioned I ftopped up with bread, and ftrewed over with duft, fo as to prevent all fufpicious appearance. My labour under this was continued with lefs precaution, and I had foon worked through my nine-inch planks. Under them I came to a fine white fand, on which the Star-Fort was built. My chips I carefully diftributed beneath the boards. If I had not help from without, I could proceed no further, for to dig were ufelefs, unlefs I could rid myfelf of my rubbifh. Gefhardt fupplied me with fome ells of cloth, of which I made long narrow bags, ftuffed them with earth, and paffed them between the iron bars, to Gefhardt, who, as often as he was on guard, fcattered or conveyed away their contents.

Furnifhed with room to fecrete them under the floor, I obtained more

inftru-

inftruments, together with a pair of piftols, powder, ball, and a bayonet.

I now difcovered that the foundation of my prifon, inftead of two, was funk four feet deep. Time, labour, and patience, were all neceffary to break out, unheard, and undifcovered; but few things are impoffible, where refolution is not wanting.

The hole I made was obliged to be four feet deep, correfponding with the foundation, and wide enough to kneel and ftoop in; the laying down on the floor to work, the continual ftooping to throw out the earth, the narrow fpace in which all muft be performed, thefe made the labour incredible; and, after this daily labour, all things were to be replaced, and my chains again refumed, which, alone, required fome hours to effect. My greateft aid was in the wax candles, and light I had procured; but as Gefhardt

hardt ſtood centinel only once a fortnight, my work was much delayed; the centinels were forbidden to ſpeak to me under pain of death: and I was too fearful of being betrayed to dare to ſeek new aſſiſtance.

Being without a ſtove, I ſuffered much this winter from cold, yet my heart was chearful, as I ſaw the probability of freedom; and all were aſtoniſhed to find me in ſuch good ſpirits.

Gefhardt, alſo, brought me ſupplies of proviſions, chiefly conſiſting of ſauſages and ſalt meats, ready dreſſed, which increaſed my ſtrength, and, when I was not digging, I wrote ſatires and verſes: thus time was employed, and I contented, even in priſon.

Lulled into ſecurity, an accident happened, that will appear almoſt incredible, and by which every hope was nearly fruſtrated.

Gefhardt had been working with

me,

me, and was relieved in the morning.
As I was replacing the window, which
I was obliged to remove on these
occasions, it fell out of my hand, and
three of the glass panes were broken.
Gefhardt was not to return till guard
was again relieved; I had, therefore,
no opportunity of speaking with him,
or concerting any mode of repair.
I remained nearly an hour conjec-
turing and hesitating, for, certainly,
had the broken window been seen, as
it was impossible I should reach it
when fettered, I should, immediately, have been more rigidly examined,
and the false grating must have been
discovered.

I, therefore, came to a resolution,
and spoke to the centinel, who was
amusing himself with whittling, thus:
" My good fellow, have pity, not
" upon me, but upon your com-
" rades, who, should you refuse,
" will certainly be executed: I will
" throw

" throw you thirty piftoles through
" the window, if you will do me a
" fmall favour." He remained fome
moments filent, and at laft anfwered,
in a low voice, " What! have you
" money then ?" — I, immediately,
counted thirty piftoles, and threw
them through the window. He
afked to know what he was to do:
I told my difficulty, and gave him
the fize of the panes, in paper. The
man, fortunately, was bold and prudent. The door of the palifadoes,
through the negligence of the officer, had not been fhut that day : he
prevailed on one of his comrades to
ftand centinel for him, during half
an hour, while he, mean time, ran
into the town, and procured the glafs,
on the receipt of which I inftantly
threw him out ten more piftoles.
Before the hour of noon and vifitation came, every thing was once
more reinftated, my glaziery performed

formed to a miracle, and the life of my worthy Gefhardt preserved!—Such is the power of money in this world! This is a very remarkable incident, for I never spoke after to the man who did me this signal service.

Gefhardt's alarm may easily be imagined: he, some days after, returned to his post, and was the more aftonished as he knew the centinel who had done me this good office; that he had five children, and was a man moft to be depended on by his officers, of any one in the whole grenadier company.

I now continued my labour, and found it very poffible to break out under the foundation; but Gefhardt had been fo terrified, by the late accident, that he ftarted a thoufand difficulties, in proportion as my end was more nearly accomplifhed; and, at the moment when I wifhed to

con-

concert with him the means of flight, he perfisted it was neceffary to find additional help, to efcape in fafety, and not bring both him and myfelf to deftruction.—At length, we came to the following determination, which, however, after eight months inceffant labour paft, render-ed my whole project abortive.

I wrote once more to Ruckhardt, at Vienna; fent him a new affignment for money, and defired he would again repair to Gummern, where he fhould wait fix feveral nights, with two fpare horfes, on the glacis of Klofterbergen, at the time appointed, every thing being prepared for flight. Within thefe fix days, Gefhardt would have found means, either in rotation, or by ex-changing the guard, to have been with me. Alas! the fweet hope of again beholding the face of the fun, of once more obtaining my freedom,

en-

endured but three days: Providence thought proper otherwife to ordain. Gefhardt fent his wife to Gummern, with the letter, and this filly woman told the poft-mafter her hufband had a lawfuit at Vienna, that, therefore, fhe begged he would take particular care of the letter, for which purpofe fhe flipped ten rix-dollars into his hand.

This unexpected liberality raifed the fufpicions of the Saxon poftmafter, who, therefore, opened the letter, read the contents, and, inftead of fending it to Vienna, or at leaft, to the general poftmafter at Drefden, he preferred the traiterous act of taking it, himfelf, to the governor of Magdeburg, who then, as at prefent, was Prince Ferdinand of Brunfwic.

What were my terrors, what my defpair, when I beheld the Prince himfelf, about three o'clock in the

after-

afternoon, enter my prifon, with his attendants, prefent my letter, and afk, in an authoritative voice, who had carried it to Gummern. — My anfwer was, " I knew not." Strict fearch was immediately made, by fmiths, carpenters, and mafons, and, after half an hour's examination, they difcovered neither my hole, nor the manner in which I difencumbered myfelf of my chains: they only faw that the middle grating, in the aperture where the light was admitted, had been removed. This was boarded up the next day, and only a fmall air-hole left, of about fix inches diameter.

The Prince began to threaten; I perfifted I had never feen the centinel, who had rendered me this fervice, nor afked his name. Seeing his attempts all ineffectual, the governor, in a milder tone, faid, "You have " ever complained, Baron Trenck,

" of

" of not having hitherto been legally
" fentenced, or heard in your own
" defence; I give you my word of
" honour, this you fhall be, and, alfo,
" that you fhall be releafed from
" your fetters, if you will only tell
" me who took your letter." To this
I replied, with all the fortitude of
innocence,——" Every body knows,
" my Lord, I have never deferved
" the treatment I have met with, in
" my country. My heart is irre-
" proachable. I feek to recover
" my liberty by every means in my
" power; but were I capable of be-
" traying the man whofe compaf-
" fion has induced him to fuccour
" my diftrefs; were I the coward
" that could purchafe happinefs at
" his expence, I then fhould, indeed,
" deferve to wear thefe chains with
" which I am loaded. For myfelf,
" do with me what you pleafe; yet
" remember I am not wholly def-
                              " titute

" titute, I am ftill a captain in the
" Imperial fervice, and a defcend-
" ant of the houfe of Trenck."

Prince Ferdinand ftood, for a moment, unable to anfwer, then renewed
his threats, and left my dungeon.
I have been fince told that, when he
was out of hearing, he faid to thofe
round him, " I pity his hard fate,
" and cannot but admire his ftrength
" of mind!"

I muft here remark that, when we
remember the ufual circumfpection
of this great man, we are obliged to
wonder at his imprudence in holding a converfation of fuch a kind
with me, which lafted a confiderable
time, in the prefence of the guard.
The foldiers of the whole garrifon
had afterward the utmoft confidence,
as they were convinced I would not
meanly devote others to deftruction,
that I might benefit myfelf. This

was

was the way to gain me efteem and intercourfe among the men, efpecially as the Duke had faid he knew I muft have money concealed, for that I had diftributed fome to the centinels.

He had fcarcely been gone an hour before I heard a noife near my prifon. I liftened—What could it be ? I heard talking, and learned a grenadier had hanged himfelf to the palifadoes of my prifon!

The officer of the guard, and the town-major, again entered my dungeon to fetch a lanthorn they had forgotten, and the officer, at going out, told me, in a whifper, " One of " your affociates has juft hanged " himfelf."

It is impoffible to impart my terror or fenfations; I believed it could be only my kind, my honeft Gefhardt. After many gloomy thoughts, and lamenting the unhappy end of fo worthy a fellow, I began to recollect what the prince had promifed me, if I would difcover my accomplice. I knocked at the door, defired to fpeak to the officer; he came to the window, and afked what I wanted; I requefted he would inform the governor that, if he would fend me light, pen, ink, and paper, I would difcover my whole fecret.

Thefe were accordingly fent; an hour's time was granted; the door was fhut, and I left alone. I fat myfelf down, began to write on my night-table, and was about to infert the name of Gefhardt, but my blood thrilled, and fhrunk back to my heart. I fhuddered, rofe, went to the aperture of the window, and cal-led, " Is there no man who, in com-" paffion, will tell me the name of " him who has hanged himfelf, that

6 " I may

" I may deliver many others from
" deſtruction !" The window was
not nailed up till the next day, I,
therefore, wrapped five piſtoles in a
paper, threw them out, called to the
centinel, and ſaid, " Friend, take
" theſe, and ſave thy comrades; or,
" go, betray me, and bring down
" innocent blood upon thy head !"

The paper was taken up ; a pauſe
of ſilence enſued; I heard ſighs, and,
preſently after, a low voice ſaid, " His
" name is Schütz, he belonged to the
" company of Ripps."——I had
never heard the name before, or
known the man, but I, however,
immediately wrote Schütz, inſtead
of Gefhardt. Having finiſhed the
letter, I called the lieutenant, who
took that and the light away, and
again barred up the door of my dungeon. The duke, however, ſuſpected there muſt be ſome colluſion,

and every thing remained in the fame
ftate ; I obtained neither hearing nor
court-martial. I learned, in the
fequel, the following circumftances,
which will difplay the truth of this
apparently incredible ftory.

While I was imprifoned in the
citadel, a centinel came to the poft
under my window, curfed and blaf-
phemed, exclaimed aloud—" Damn
" the Pruffian fervice ! If Trenck
" only knew my mind, he would
" not long continue in his infernal
" hole !" I entered into difcourfe
with him, and he told me, if I could
give him money to purchafe a boat,
in which he might crofs the Elbe,
he would foon make my doors fly
open, and fet me free.

Money at that time I had none ;
but I gave him a diamond fhirt
buckle, worth five hundred florins,
which I had concealed. I never
heard

heard more from this man; he spoke to me no more. He often stood centinel over me, which I knew by his Westphalian dialect, and I as often addressed myself to him, but ineffectually, he would make no an-swer.

This Schütz must have sold my buckle, and let his riches be seen, for, when the duke left me, the lieutenant on guard said to him— " You must, certainly, be the rascal " who carried Trenck's letter; you " have, for some time past, spent much " money, and we have seen you with " louis-d'ors. How came you by " them?" Schütz was terrified, his conscience accused him, he ima-gined I should betray him, he hav-ing deceived me. He, therefore, in the first agonies of despair, came to the palisades, and hung himself before the door of my dungeon.

F 3

How

How wonderful is the hand of Providence! The wicked man fell a facrifice to his crime, after having efcaped a whole year, and the faithful, the benevolent-hearted, Gefhardt was thereby faved.

The centinels were now doubled, that any intercourfe with them might be rendered more difficult. Gefhardt again ftood guard, but he had fcarcely opportunity, without danger, to fpeak a few words: he thanked me for having preferved him, wifhed me better fortune, and told me the garrifon, in a few days, would take the field.

This was dreadful news: my whole plan was deftroyed at a breath. I, however, foon recovered frefh hopes. The hole I had funken was not difcovered: I had five hundred florins, candles, and implements.

The feven years war broke out

about

about a week after, and the regiments took the field. Major Weyner came, for the laſt time, and committed me to the care of the new major of the militia, Bruckhauſen, who was one of the moſt ſurly and ſtupid of men. I ſhall often have occaſion to mention this man.

All the majors and lieutenants of the guard, who had treated me with compaſſion and eſteem, now departed, and I became an old priſoner in a new world. I acquired greater confidence, however, by remembering that both officers and men in the militia were much eaſier to gain over than in the regulars; the truth of which opinion was ſoon confirmed to me.

Four lieutenants were appointed, with their men, to mount guard at the Star-Fort in turn, and, before

F 4

a year

a year had paſſed, three of them were in my intereſt.

The regiments had ſcarcely taken the field ere the new governor, General Borck, entered my priſon like what he was, an imperious, cruel tyrant. The King, in giving him the command, had informed him he muſt anſwer for my perſon with his head; he, therefore, had full power to treat me with whatever ſeverity he pleaſed.

Borck was a ſtupid man, of an unfeeling heart, the ſlave of deſpotic orders, and, as often as he thought it poſſible I might rid myſelf of my fetters, and eſcape, his heart palpitated with fear. In addition to this, he conſidered me as the vileſt of men and traitors, ſeeing his King had condemned me to impriſonment ſo cruel, and his barbarity toward me was thus the effect of character,

and

and meannefs of foul. He entered my dungeon not as an officer, to vifit a brother officer in mifery, but as an executioner to a felon. Smiths then made their appearance, and a monftrous iron collar, of a hand's breadth, was put round my neck, and connected with the chains of the feet by additional heavy links, as may be feen in the plate. My window was walled up, except a fmall air-hole. He even, at length, took away my bed, gave me no ftraw, and quitted me with a thou-fand revilings on the Emprefs Queen, her whole army, and myfelf. In words, however, I was little in his debt, and he was enraged even to madnefs.

What my fituation was under this additional load of tyranny, and the command of a man fo void of hu-man pity, the reader muft imagine.

F 5
My

My greateſt good fortune conſiſted in the ability I ſtill had to diſencumber myſelf of all the irons that were connected with the ancle-rims, and the proviſion I had of light, paper, and implements; and, though it was, apparently, impoſſible I ſhould break out undiſcovered by both centinels, yet had I the remaining hope of gaining ſome officer, by money, who, as in Glatz, ſhould aſſiſt my eſcape.

Had the commands of the King been literally obeyed, eſcape would have been wholly impoſſible; for, by this, all communication would have been cut totally off with the centinels. To this effect the four keys of the four doors were each to be kept by different perſons; one with the governor, another with the town-major, the third with the major of the day, and the fourth with the lieutenant

of

of the guard. I never could have found opportunity to have spoken with any one of them singly. These commands, at firſt, were rigidly obſerved, with this exception, that the governor made his appearance only every week. Magdeburg became ſo full of priſoners that the town-major was obliged to deliver up his key to the major of the day, and the governor's viſitations wholly ſubſided, the citadel being an Engliſh mile and a half diſtant from the Star-Fort.

General Walrabe, * who had been a priſoner ever ſince the year 1746, was alſo at the Star-Fort, but he had

F 6

apart-

* Walrave (or Walrabe) had long been ſuſpected of partiality to Auſtria, he being a bigotted catholic. He was, at length, betrayed by a miſtreſs, for whoſe huſband (for ſhe was married) he had obtained the dignity of counſellor. Frederic, when he granted

the·

apartments, and three thousand rix-dollars a year. The major of the day and the officers of the guard dined with him daily, and generally ftaid till evening. Either from compaffion, or a concurrence of fortunate circumftances, thefe gentlemen entrufted the keys to the lieutenant on guard, by which means I could fpeak with each of them alone when they made their vifit, and they themfelves, at length, fought thefe opportunities. My confequent undertakings I fhall relate with all brevity, that I may not fatigue the reader with all the arts and inven-

the title, told Walrave it certainly became the miftrefs of a general to have a counfellor for a hufband. He was fuperintendent of the fortifications, and was confined, not, according to Fifcher, in 1746, but in 1748, in a prifon himfelf had built at Magdeburg. T.

See **Fifcher Gefchichte Fried. II. Theil I. S. 265.** .

tions

tions of a wretched prifoner endeavouring to efcape.

Borck had felected three majors
and four lieutenants only for this
fervice, as thofe he beft could truft.
My fituation was truly deplorable.
The enormous iron round my neck
pained me, and prevented motion,
and I durft not attempt to difengage
myfelf from the pendent chains till
I had, for fome months, carefully obferved the mode of their examination, and which parts they fuppofed
were perfectly fecure. The cruelty of
depriving me of my bed was ftill
greater: I was obliged to fit upon the
bare ground, and lean with my head
againft the damp wall. The chains
that defcended from the neck-collar
were obliged to be fupported firft
with one hand, and then with the
other, for, if thrown behind, they
would have ftrangled me, and, if

hanging

hanging forward, occafioned moft exceffive headachs. The bar between my hands held one down while leaning on my elbow; I fupported with the other my chains, and this fo benumbed the mufcles, and prevented circulation, that I could perceive my arms fenfibly wafte away. The little fleep I could have in fuch a fituation may eafily be fuppofed, and, at length, body and mind funk under this accumulation of miferable fuffering, and I fell ill of a burning fever.

The tyrant Borck was inexorable; he wifhed to expedite my death, and rid himfelf of his troubles and his terrors. Here did I experience what was the lamentable condition of a fick prifoner, without bed, refrefhment, or aid from human being. Reafon, fortitude, heroifm, all the noble qualities of the mind, decay

when

when the corporal faculties are dif-
eafed, and the remembrance of my
fufferings, at this dreadful moment,
ftill agitates, ftill inflames, my blood
fo as almoft to prevent an attempt
to defcribe what they were.

Yet hope had not totally forfaken
me. Deliverance feemed poffible,
efpecially, fhould peace enfue ; and I
fuftained, perhaps, what mortal man
never bore, except myfelf, being,
as I was, provided with piftols, or any
fuch immediate mode of difpatch.

I continued ill about two months,
and was fo reduced, at laft, that I had
fcarcely ftrength to lift the water-
jug to my mouth. What muft the
fufferings of that man be who fits
two months on the bare ground in
a dungeon fo damp, fo dark, fo horrible, without bed or ftraw, his
limbs loaded as mine were, with no
refrefhment but dry ammunition
bread,

bread, without so much as a drop of broth, without physic, without consoling friend, and who, under all these afflictions, must trust, for his recovery, to the efforts of nature alone !

Sickness itself is sufficient to humble the mightiest mind; what then is sickness, with such addition of torment? The burning fever, the violent headachs, my neck, swelled and inflamed with the irons, enraged me almost to madness. The fever, and the fetters, together, flead my body so that it appeared like one continued wound—Enough ! Enough ! ——The malefactor extended living on the wheel, to whom the cruel executioner refuses the last stroke, the blow of death, must yet, in some short period, expire: he suffers nothing I did not then suffer, and these my excruciating pangs conti-

nued

nued two dreadful months————
Yet, can it be fuppofed ? There came
a day !————A day of horror, when
thefe mortal pangs were, beyond imagination, increafed ! I fat, fcorched
with this intolerable fever, in which
nature and death were contending,
and, when attempting to· quench
my burning entrails with cold water,
the jug dropped from my feeble
hands, and broke ! I had four and
twenty hours to remain without water. So intolerable, fo devouring,
was my thirft, I could have drank
human blood ! Ay, in my madnefs,
had it been the blood of my father !

*　*　*　*　*　*　*　*　*　*

Willingly would I have feized my
piftols, but ftrength had forfaken
me; I could not open the place I
was obliged to render fo fecure.

My vifitors, next day, fuppofed
me gone at laft——I lay motionlefs,
with

with my tongue out of my mouth. They poured water down my throat, and found life.

Oh God! Oh God! How pure, how delicious, how exquifite, was this water!——My infatiable thirft foon emptied the jug; they filled it anew, bade me farewel, hoped death would foon relieve my mortal fufferings, and departed.

The lamentable ftate in which I lay, at length, became fo much the fubject of general converfation that all the ladies of the town united with the officers, and prevailed on the tyrant, Borck, to reftore me my bed.

Oh Nature, what are thy operations? From the day I drank water in fuch excefs, I gathered ftrength, and, to the aftonifhment of every one, foon recovered.——I had moved the heart of the officer who infpected my prifon;

prifon; and, after fix months, fix cruel months, of added mifery, the day of hope again began to dawn.

One of the majors of the day en-trufted his key to Lieutenant Sonn-tag, who came alone, fpoke in confi-dence, and related his own fituation, complained of his debts, his poverty, his neceffities; and I made him a.pre-fent of twenty-five louis-d'ors, for which he was fo grateful that our friendfhip became unfhaken.

The three lieutenants all com-miferated me, and would fit hours with me, when a certain major had the infpection; and he himfelf, after a time, would even pafs half the day with me. He, too, was poor; and I gave him a draft for three thou-fand florins: hence new projects took birth.

Money became neceffary; I had difperfed all I poffeffed, a hundred
florins

florins excepted, among the officers. The eldeft fon of Captain K——, who officiated as major, had been cafhiered: his father complained to me of his diftrefs, and I fent him to my fifter, not far from Berlin, from whom he received a hundred ducats. He returned, and related her joy at hearing from me. He found her exceedingly ill, and fhe informed me, in a few lines, that my misfortunes, and the treachery of Weingarten, had entailed poverty upon her, and an illnefs which had endured more than two years. She wifhed me a happy deliverance from my chains, and, in expectation of death, committed her children to my protection. She, however, grew better, and married a fecond time, Colonel Pape; but died in the year 1758. I fhall forbear to relate her hiftory; it, indeed, does no honour

to

to the afhes of Frederic, and would
but lefs difpofe my own heart to forgivenefs, by reviving the memory
of her oppreffions and griefs.

K——n returned, happy, with the
money: all things were concerted
with the father. I wrote to the
Countefs Beftuchef, alfo to the
Grand Duke, afterwards Peter III.
recommended the young foldier,
and entreated every poffible fuccour
for myfelf.

K——n departed, through Hamburg, for Peterfburg, where, in confequence of my recommendation, he
became a captain, and, in a fhort time,
major. He took his meafures fo
well that I, by the intervention of his
father, and a Hamburg merchant,
received two thoufand rubles from
the Countefs, while the fervice he
rendered me made his own fortune
in Ruffia.

To

To old K——, who was as poor as he was honeſt, I gave three hundred ducats; and he, till death, continued my grateful friend. I diſtributed nearly as much to the other officers; and matters proceeded ſo far that Lieutenant Glotin gave back the keys to the major without locking my priſon, himſelf paſſing half the night with me. Money was given to the guard to drink, and thus every thing ſucceeded to my wiſh, and the tyrant, Borck, was deceived. I had a ſupply of light; had books, newſpapers, and my days paſſed ſwiftly away. I read, I wrote, I buſied myſelf ſo thoroughly that I almoſt forgot I was a priſoner.—— When, indeed, the ſurly, dull blockhead, Major Bruckhauſen, had the inſpection, every thing muſt be carefully reinſtated. Major Z——, the ſecond of the three, was alſo wholly mine.

mine. He was particularly attached to me, for I had promifed to marry his daughter, and, fhould I die in prifon, bequeathed him a legacy of ten thoufand florins.

Lieutenant Sonntag got falfe hand-cuffs made for me, that were fo wide I could eafily draw my hands out; the lieutenants, only, examined my irons; the new hand-cuffs were made perfectly fimilar to the old, and Bruckhaufen had too much ftupidity to remark any difference.

The remainder of my chains I could difencumber myfelf of at plea-fure. When I exercifed myfelf, I held them in my hands, that the centinels might be deceived by their clanking. The neck-iron was the only one I durft not remove; it was, likewife, too ftrongly rivetted. I filed through the upper link of the pen-dent chain however, by which means

I could

I could take it off, and this I concealed with bread in the manner
before mentioned.

So could I difencumber myfelf
of moft of my fetters, and fleep at
eafe. I again obtained faufages and
cold meat, and thus my fituation,
bad as it ftill was, became lefs miferable. — Liberty, ftill, however,
was moft defirable: but, alas! not
one of the three lieutenants had the
courage of a Schell: Saxony, too,
was in the hands of the Pruffians, and
flight, therefore, more dangerous.—
Perfuafion was in vain, with men
determined to rifk nothing, but, if
they went, to go in fafety. Will,
indeed, was not wanting in Glotin
and Sonntag; but the firft was a
poltroon, and the latter a man of
fcruples, who, likewife, thought this
ftep might be the ruin of his brother in Berlin.

The

The centinels were doubled, therefore my escape through my hole,
which had been two years dug,
could not, unperceived by them, be
effected; still less could I, in face of
the guard, clamber the twelve-feet
high palisadoes. The following labour, therefore, though Herculean,
was undertaken.

Lieutenant Sonntag, measuring
the interval, between the hole I had
dug and the entrance of the gallery
in the principal rampart, found it to
be thirty-seven feet. Into this, it was
possible, I might, by mining, penetrate. The difficulty of the enter-
prise was lessened by the nature of
the ground, a fine white sand. —
Could I reach the gallery, my freedom was certain. I had been informed how many steps to the right
or left must be taken, to find the

door that led to the second rampart:
and, on the day when I should be
ready for flight, the officer was,
secretly, to leave this door open. I
had light, and mining tools, and I
was further to rely on money and
my own discretion.

I began and continued this labour
about six months. I have already
noticed the difficulty of scraping out
the earth with my hands. The noise
of instruments would have been heard
by the centinels; I had scarcely
mined beyond my dungeon wall before I discovered the foundation of
the rampart was not more than a foot
deep, a capital error, certainly, in
so important a fortress. My labour
became the lighter as I could remove the foundation stones of my
dungeon, and was not obliged to
mine so deep.

My work, at first, proceeded so
rapidly

rapidly that, while I had room to throw back my fand, I was able, in one night, to gain three feet; but ere I had proceeded ten feet I difcovered all my difficulties. Before I could continue my work, I was obliged to make room for myfelf, by emptying the fand out of my hole upon the floor of the prifon, and this itfelf was an employment of fome hours. The fand was obliged to be thrown out by the hand, and, after it thus lay heaped in my prifon, muft be again returned into the hole, and I have calculated that, after I had proceeded twenty feet, I was obliged to creep under ground, in my hole, from fifteen hundred to two thoufand fathoms, within twenty-four hours, in the removal and replacing of the fand. This labour ended, care was to be taken that, in

none

none of the crevices of the floor, there might be any appearance of this fine white fand. The flooring was next to be exactly replaced, and my chains to be refumed. So fevere was the fatigue of one day, in this mode, that I was always oblig-ed to reft the three following.

To reduce my labour, as much as poffible, I was conftrained to make the paffage fo fmall that my body only had fpace to pafs, and I had not room to draw my arm back to my head. The work too muft all be done naked, otherwife the dirti-nefs of my fhirt muft have been re-marked: the fand was wet, water being found at the depth of four feet, where the ftratum of gravel began. At length, the expedient of fand bags occurred to me ; by which it might be removed out and in more expeditioufly. I obtained linen from

the

the officers, but not in fufficient quantities; fufpicions would have been excited at obferving fo much linen brought into the prifon. At laft, I took my fheets, and the ticking that inclofed my ftraw, and cut them up for fand bags, taking care to lie down on my bed, as if ill, when Bruck-haufen paid his vifits.

The labour, toward the conclu-fion, became fo intolerable as to in-cite defpondency. I frequently fat contemplating the heaps of fand, during a momentary refpite from work, and, thinking it impoffible I could have ftrength or time again to replace all things as they were, re-folving patiently to wait the con-fequence, and leave every thing in its prefent diforder. No, I can affure the reader that, to effect concealment, I have fcarcely had time, in twenty-four hours, to fit down and eat a

mor-

morfel of bread. — Recollecting, however, the prodigious efforts, and all the progrefs I had made, hope would again revive, and exhaufted ftrength return; again would I begin my labours, that I might preferve my fecret and my expectations: yet has it frequently happened that my vifitors have entered a few minutes after I had reinftated every thing in its place.

When my work was within fix or feven feet of being accomplifhed, a new misfortune happened that at once fruftrated all further attempts. I worked, as I have faid, under the foundation of the rampart near where the centinels ftood. I could difencumber myfelf of my fetters, except my neck-collar, and its pendent chain. This, as I worked, though it had been faftened, got loofe, and the clanking was heard by one of
the

the centinels about fifteen feet from
my dungeon. The officer was called, they laid their ears to the
ground, and heard me as I went
backward and forward to bring my
earth bags. This was reported the
next day, and the major, who was
my beſt friend, with the town-major,
and a ſmith and maſon, entered my
priſon. I was terrified. The lieutenant, by a ſign, gave me to under-
ſtand I was diſcovered. An examination was begun, but the officers
would not ſee, and the ſmith and
maſon found every thing, as they
thought, ſafe. Had they examined
my bed, they would have ſeen the
ticking and ſheets were gone.

The town-major was a dull man,
was perſuaded the thing was impoſſible, and ſaid to the centinel,
" Blockhead ! You have heard ſome
" mole under ground, and not

          " Trenck.

" Trenck. How, indeed, could it
" be, that he fhould work under
" ground at fuch a diftance from
" his dungeon ?" Here the fcrutiny
ended.

There was now no time for delay.
Had they altered their hour of coming, they muft have found me at
work; but this, during ten years,
never happened, for the governor
and town-major were ftupid men,
and the others, wifhing me all fuccefs, were wilfully blind. In a few
days I could have broken out, but,
when prepared, wifhed to wait for
the vifitation day of the man who
had treated me fo tyrannically,
Bruckhaufen, that his own negligence might be evident, but this
man, though he wanted underftanding, did not want good fortune. He
was ill for fome time, and his duty
devolved on K———.

He

He recovered, and, the visitation being over, the doors were no sooner barred than I began my supposed last labour. I had only three feet farther to proceed, and it was no longer neceffary I should bring out the fand, I having room enough to throw it behind me. What my anxiety was, what my exertions were, may well be imagined. My evil genius, however, had decreed that the fame centinel, who had heard me before, should be that day on guard. He was piqued, by vanity, to prove he was not the blockhead he had been called : he, therefore, again laid his ear to the ground, and again heard me burrowing. He called his comrades firft, next the major : he came, and heard me likewife ; accordingly, they went without the palifadoes, and heard me working near the door, at which place I was to break

into

into the gallery. This door they immediately opened, entered the gallery
with lanthorns, and waited to catch
the hunted fox when unearthed.

Through the firſt ſmall breach I
made, I perceived a light, and ſaw
the heads of thoſe who were expecting me. This was, indeed, a thunder
ſtroke!—I crept back, made my
way through the ſand I had caſt behind me, and awaited my fate with
ſhuddering! I had ſtill the preſence
of mind to conceal my piſtols, candles, paper, and ſome money, under
the floor, which I could remove.—
The money was diſpoſed of in various holes, well concealed, alſo between the pannels of the doors; and,
under different cracks in the floor, I
hid my ſmall files and knives.

Scarcely were theſe diſpoſed of
before the doors reſounded; the floor

was

was covered with fand and fand bags; my hand-cuffs, however, and the feparating bar, I had haftily refumed, that they might fuppofe I had worked with them on, which they were filly enough to credit, highly to my future advantage.

No man was more bufy on this occafion than the brutal and ftupid Bruckhaufen, who put many interrogatories, to which I made no reply, except affuring him that I fhould have completed my work fome days fooner, had it not been his good fortune to fall fick, and that this only had been the caufe of my failure.

The man was abfolutely terrified with apprehenfion : he began to fear me, grew more polite, and even fuppofed nothing was impoffible to me.

It

It was too late to remove the sand, therefore, the lieutenant and guard continued with me, so that this night, at least, I did not want company. When the morning came, the hole was first filled and walled up; the planking was renewed. The tyrant Borck was ill, and could not come, otherwise my treatment would have been still more lamentable. The smiths had ended before the evening, and the irons were heavier than ever. The foot chains, instead of being fastened as before, were screwed and rivetted; all things else remained as formerly. They were employed in the flooring till the next day, so that I could not sleep, and at last I sank down with weariness.

The greatest of my misfortunes was, they again deprived me of my bed, because I had cut it up for

sand

fand bags. Before the doors were barred, Bruckhäufen, and another major examined my body very narrowly. They often had afked me, where I concealed all my implements? My anfwer was, " Gentle-
" men, Beelzebub is my beft and
" moft intimate friend ; he. brings
" me every thing I want, fupplies
" me with light, we play whole
" nights at piquet, and, guard me
" as you pleafe, he will finally deli-
" ver me out of your power."

Some were aftonifhed, others laughed. At length, as they were barring the laft door, I called,
" Come back, gentlemen ! You have
" forgotten fomething of great im-
" portance." In the interim I had taken up one of my hidden files.
When they returned, " Look ye,
" gentlemen," faid I, " here is a proof
" of the friendfhip Beelzebub has
" for

" for me; he has brought me this
" in a twinkling." Again they
examined, and again they shut their
doors. While they were so doing,
I took out a knife, and ten louis-d'ors,
called, and they returned, grumbling
curses: I then showed them the knife
and the louis-d'ors. Their conster-
nation was excessive; and I diverted
my misfortunes, by jesting at such
blundering, short sighted, keepers.
It was soon rumoured through
Magdeburg, especially among the
simple and the vulgar, that I was a
magician, to whom the devil brought
all I asked.

One Major Holtzkammer, a very
selfish man, profited by this report.
A foolish citizen had offered him
fifty dollars, if he might only be
permitted to see me through the
door, being very desirous to have a
peep at a wizard. Holtzkammer

told

told me, and we jointly determined to fport with his credulity. The major gave me a mafk, with a monftrous nofe, which I put on when the doors were opening, and threw myfelf into a heroic attitude. The affrighted Burger drew back, but Holtzkammer ftopped him, and faid, have patience but for fome quarter of an hour, and you fhall fee he will affume quite a different countenance. The Burger waited, my mafk was thrown by, and my face appeared whitened with chalk, and made ghaftly. The Burger again fhrank back; Holtzkammer kept him in converfation, and I affumed a third farcical form. I tied my hair under my nofe, and a pewter difh to my breaft, and, when the door a third time opened, I thundered, "Begone, "rafcals, or I'll fet your necks "awry!" They both ran, and the

filly

filly Burger, eafed of his fifty dollars, fcampered firft.

The major in vain laid his injunctions on the Burger never to reveal what he had beheld, it being a breach of duty in him to admit any perfon whatever to the fight of me. In a few days, the necromancer Trenck was the theme of every alehoufe in Magdeburg, and the perfon was named who had feen me change my form thrice in the fpace of one hour. Many falfe and ridiculous circumftances were added, and at laft the ftory reached the governor's ears. The citizen was cited, and offered to take his oath to the truth of what himfelf, and the major, had feen. Holtzkammer, accordingly, fuffered a fevere reprimand, and was fome days put under arreft. We frequently laughed, however, at this adventure, which had rendered me

fo

fo much the fubject of converfation.
Miraculous reports were the more
eafily credited, becaufe no one could
comprehend how, in defpite of the
load of irons I carried, and all the
vigilance of my guards, I fhould be
continually able to make new attempts, while thofe appointed to examine my dungeon feemed, as it
were, blinded and bewildered. A
proof, this, how eafy it is to deceive
the credulous, and whence have originated witchcraft, prophecies, and
miracles.

My laft undertaking had employed
me more than twelve months, and
fo weakened me that I appeared
little better than a fkeleton. Notwithftanding the greatnefs of my
fpirit, I fhould have funken into defpondency, at feeing an end, like this,
to all my labours, had I not ftill che-
rifhed a fecret hope of efcaping,
founded

founded on the friends I had gained among the officers.

I soon felt the effects of the loss of my bed, and was a second time attacked by a violent fever, which would this time, certainly, have consumed me, had not the officers, unknown to the governor, treated me with all possible compassion. Bruckhausen, alone, continued my enemy, and the slave of his orders: on his day of examination, rules and commands, in all their rigour, were observed, nor durst I free myself from my irons, till I had for some weeks remarked those parts on which he invariably fixed his attention. I then cut through the. link, .and closed up the vacancy with bread. My hands I could always draw out, especially, after illness had consumed the flesh off my bones. Half a year had elapsed, before I had recovered

suffi-

fufficient ftrength to undertake, anew,
labours like the paft.

Neceffity, at length, taught me
the means of driving Bruckhaufen
from my dungeon, and of inducing
him to commit his office to another.
I learnt his olfactory nerves were
fomewhat delicate, and, whenever I
heard the doors unbar, I took care
to make a ftir in my night-table.
This made him give back, and at
length he would come no farther
than the door. Such are the hard
expedients of a poor, unhappy, prifoner !

One day he came, bloated with
pride, juft after a courier had brought
the news of victory, and fpoke of
the Auftrians, and the auguft perfon
of the Emprefs-Queen, with fo
much virulence that, at laft, enraged
almoft to madnefs, I fnatched the
fword of an officer from its fheath,

and

and should certainly have ended him,
had he not made a hasty retreat.
From that day forward he durst no
more come without guards to examine the dungeon. Two men always preceded him, with their bayonets fixed, and their pieces presented,
behind whom he stood at the door.
This was another fortunate incident,
as I dreaded only his examination.

The following anecdote will afford
a specimen of this man's understand-
ing. While digging in the earth, I
found a cannon ball, and laid it in
the middle of my prison. When
he came to examine—" What, in
" the name of God, is that ?" said
he. " It is a part of the ammu-
" nition," answered I, " that my
" Familiar brings me. The cannon
" will be here anon, and you will
" then see fine sport !" He was
astonished, told this to others, nor
could

could conceive fuch a ball might by any natural means enter my pri-fon.

I wrote a fatire on him, when the late Landgrave of Heffe-Caffel was governor of Magdeburg, and I had permiffion to write, as will hereafter appear: the Landgrave gave it to him, to read himfelf; and, fo grofs was his conception, that, though his own phrafeology was introduced, part of his hiftory, and his character painted, yet did he not perceive the jeft, but laughed heartily with the hearers. The Landgrave was highly diverted, and, after I obtained my freedom, reftored me the manufcript, written in my own blood.

About the time that my laft at-tempt at efcaping failed, General Krufemarck came to my prifon, whom I had formerly lived with in habits of intimacy, when cornet of the body-guard.

guard. Without teftifying friendfhip, efteem, or compaffion, he afked,
among other things, in an authoritative tone, how I could employ
my time to prevent tedioufnefs. I
anfwered in as haughty a mood as
he interrogated; for never could mif-
fortune bend my mind. I told him,
" I always could find fources of en-
" tertainment in my own thoughts,
" and that, as for my dreams, I ima-
" gined they would, at leaft, be as
" peaceful and pleafant as thofe of
" my oppreffors,"—" Had you, in
" time," replied he, " curbed this
" fervor of yours, had you afked
" pardon of the King, perhaps you
" would have been in very different
" circumftances; but he, who has
" committed an offence in which he
" obftinately perfifts, endeavouring
" only to obtain freedom by feduc-
" ing

" ing men from their duty, deferves
" no better fate."

Juftly was my anger roufed !—
" Sir," anfwered I, " you are a gene-
" ral of the King of Pruffia, I am an
" Auftrian captain.—My royal mif-
" trefs will protect, perhaps deliver
" me, or at leaft revenge my death.
" I have a confcience void of re-
" proach. You, yourfelf, well know
" I have not deferved thefe chains.
" I place my hope in time, and the
" juftnefs of my caufe, calumniated
" and condemned, as I have been,
" without legal fentence or hearing.
" In fuch a fituation the philofopher
" will always be able to brave and
" defpife the tyrant."

He departed with threats, and his
laft words were—" The bird fhall
" foon be taught to fing another
" tune."—The effects of this cour-
teous vifit were foon felt. An order

came

came that I should be prevented sleeping, and that the centinels should call, and wake me, every quarter of an hour, which dreadful order was immediately executed.

This was, indeed, a punishment intolerable to nature! Yet did custom, at length, teach me to answer in my sleep. Four years did this unheard-of cruelty continue! The noble Landgrave of Hesse-Cassel, at length, put an end to it, a year before I was released from my dungeon, and once again, in mercy, suffered me to sleep in peace.

Under this new affliction I wrote an Elegy, which may be found in the second volume of my works, a few lines of which I shall cite.

Wake me, ye guards, for hark, the quarter strikes!
Sport with my woes, laugh loud at my miseries!
Hearken if you hear my chains clank! Knock! Beat!
Of an inexorable Tyrant be ye

Th'

Th' inexorable inftruments! Wake me, ye flaves;
Ye do but as you're bade.   Soon fhall he lie
Sleeplefs, or, dreaming, the fpectres of confcience
Behold and fhriek, who me deprives of reft.

Wake me! Again the quarter ftrikes! Call, loud!
Rip up all my bleeding wounds, and fhrink not!
Yet, think, 'tis I that anfwer, God that hears!
To every wretch in chains fleep is permitted :
I, I, alone, am robb'd of this laft refuge
Of finking nature! Hark! Again they thunder!
Again they iterate' yells of Trenck and death!

Peace to thy anger, peace thou fuffering heart,
Nor indignant beat, adding tenfold pangs to pain.

Ye burthened limbs arife from momentary
Slumbers! Shake your chains! Murmur not, but rife!
And ye! Watch-dogs of power! let loofe your rage :
Fear not, for I am helplefs, unprotected.
And, yet, not fo—The noble mind, within
Itfelf, refources finds innumerable.
Thou, Oh God, thought'ft good me t' imprifon thus;
Thou, Oh God, in thy good time, wilt me deliver,

Wake me then, nor fear! My foul flumbers not.
And who can fay but thofe who fetter me
May, ere to-morrow, groan themfelves in fetters?
Wake me! For lo! their fleep's lefs fweet than mine.
Call! Call! From night to morn, from twilight to dawn
Inceffant! Yea, in God's name, Call! Call! Call!
Amen! Amen! Thy will, Oh God, be done!
Yet furely thou at length fhalt hear my fighs!
Shalt burft my prifon doors! Shalt fhew me fair
Creation! Yea the very heav'n of heav'ns.

With whom thefe orders originated, unexampled in the hiftory
even of tyranny, I fhall not venture
to fay. The major, who was my
friend, advifed me to perfift in not
anfwering. I followed his advice,
and it produced this good effect
that we mutually forced each other
to a capitulation: they reftored me
my bed, and I was obliged to reply.

Immediately after this regulation,
the fub-governor, General Borck, my
bitter enemy, became infane, was
difpoffeffed of his poft, and Lieu-
tenant-colonel Reichmann, the benevolent friend of humanity, was made
fub-governor.

About the fame time the court
fled from Berlin, and the Queen, the
Prince of Pruffia, the Princefs Amelia, and the Margrave Henry, chofe
Magdeburg for their refidence.
Bruckhaufen grew more polite, probably,

bably, perceiving I was not wholly deferted, and that it was yet poffible I might obtain my freedom. The cruel are, ufually, cowards, and there is reafon to fuppofe Bruckhaufen was actuated by his fears to treat me with greater refpect.

The worthy new governor had not, indeed, the power to lighten my chains, or alter the general regulations: what he could he did. If he did not command, he connived at the doors being, occafionally, at firft, and, at length, daily, kept open fome hours, to admit day-light and frefh air. After a time they were open the whole day, and only clofed by the officers when they returned from their vifit to Walrabe.

Having light, I began to carve, with a nail, on the pewter cup in which I drank, fatirical verfes and various figures, and attained fo

much

much perfection that my cups, at laſt, were conſidered as maſter-pieces, both of engraving and invention, and were fold dear as rare curioſities. My firſt attempts were rude, as may well be imagined. My cup was carried to town, and ſhown to viſitors by the governor, who fent me another. I improved, and each of the infpecting officers wiſhed to poſſeſs one. I grew more expert, and ſpent a whole year in this employment, which thus paſſed ſwiftly away. The perfection I had now acquired obtained me the permiſſion of candle-light, and this continued till I was reſtored to freedom.

The King gave orders theſe cups ſhould all be infpected by government, becauſe I wiſhed, by my verfes and devices, to inform the world of my fate. But this command was not obeyed; the officers

made

made merchandize of my cups, and fold them, at laft, for twelve ducats each. Their value increafed fo much, when I was releafed from prifon, that they are now to be found in various mufeums throughout Europe. Twelve years ago the late Landgrave of Heffe-Caffel prefented one of them to my wife; and another came, in a very unaccountable manner, from the Queen Dowager of Pruffia, to Paris. I have given prints of both thefe, with the verfes they contained, in my works; whence it may be feen how artificially they were engraved.

A third fell into the hands of Prince Auguftus Lobkowitz, then a prifoner of war at Magdeburg, who, on his return to Vienna, prefented it to the Emperor, who placed it in his mufeum. Among other devices on this cup was a landfcape, repre-

H 3

fenting

fenting a vineyard and hufbandmen, and under it the following words: *By my labours my vineyard flourished, and I hoped to have gathered the fruit; but Ahab came. Alas! for Naboth.*

The allufion was fo pointed, both to the wrongs done me in Vienna and my fufferings in Pruffia, that it made a very ftrong impreffion on the Emprefs-Queen, who, immediately, commanded her minifter to make every exertion for my deliverance. She would, probably, at laft, have even reftored me to my eftates, had not the poffeffors of them been fo powerful, or, had fhe herfelf lived one year longer. To thefe my engraved cups was I indebted for being once more remembered at Vienna. On the fame cup, alfo, was another engraving of a bird in a cage, held by a Turk, with the following infcription: *The bird*

bird sings even in the storm; open his cage, break his fetters, ye friends of virtue, and his songs shall be the delight of your abodes!

There is another remarkable circumstance attending thefe cups. All were forbidden, under pain of death, to hold converfation with me, or to fupply me with pen and ink; yet, by this open permiffion of writing what I pleafed on pewter, was I enabled to inform the world of all I wifhed, and to prove a man of merit was oppreffed. The difficulties of this engraving will be conceived when it is remembered that I worked, by candle-light, on fhining pewter, attained the art of giving light and fhade, and, by practice, could divide a cup, into two and thirty compartments, as regularly with a ftroke of the hand as with a pair of compaffes. The writing was fo minute that it could

H 4

be

be only read with glasses. I could use but one hand, both being separated by the bar, and, therefore, held the cup between my knees. My sole instrument was a sharpened nail, yet did I write two lines on the rim only.

My labour became so excessive that I was in danger of distraction or blindness. Every body wished for cups, and I wished to oblige every body, so that I worked eighteen hours a day. The reflection of the light from the pewter was injurious to my eyes, and the labour of invention for apposite subjects and verses was most fatiguing. I had learnt only architectural drawing.

Enough of these cups, which procured me so much honour, so many advantages, and helped to shorten so many mournful hours. My greatest incumbrance was the huge

iron

iron collar, with its enormous appendages, which, when fuffered to prefs the arteries in the back of my neck, occafioned intolerable headachs. I fat too much, and a third time fell fick. A Brunfwic faufage, fecretly given me by a friend, occafioned an indigeftion, which endangered my life; a putrid fever followed, and my body was reduced to a fkeleton. Medicines, however, were conveyed to me by the officers, and, now and then, warm food.

After my recovery I again thought it neceffary to endeavour to regain my liberty. I had but forty louis-d'ors remaining, and thefe I could not get till I had firft broken up the flooring.

Lieutenant Sonntag was confumptive, and obtained his difcharge. I fupplied him with money to defray the expences of his journey, and

H 5   with

with an order that four hundred florins should be annually paid him, from my effects, till his death, or my release. I commissioned him to seek an audience from the Empress, endeavour to excite her compassion in my behalf, and to remit me four thousand florins, for which I gave a proper acquittance, by the way of Hamburg. The money-draft was addressed to my administrators, counsellors Kempf and Huttner.

But no one, alas, in Vienna wished my return : they had already begun to share my property, of which they never rendered me an account. Poor Sonntag was arrested as a spy, imprisoned, ill treated for some weeks, and, at last, when naked and destitute, received a hundred florins, and was escorted beyond the Austrian confines. The worthy man fell a shameful sacrifice to his honesty,

could

could never obtain an audience of the Emprefs, and returned, poor and miferable, on foot, to Berlin, where he was twelve months fecretly maintained by his brother, and with whom he died. He wrote an account of all this to the good Knoblauch, my Hamburg agent, and I, from my fmall ftore, fent him a hundred ducats.

How much muft I defpair of finding any place of refuge on earth, hearing accounts like thefe from Vienna!

A friend, whom I will never name, by the aid of one of the lieutenants, fecretly vifited me, and fupplied me with fix hundred ducats. The fame friend, in the year 1763, paid four thoufand florins to the imperial envoy, Baron Riedt, at Berlin, for the furthering of my freedom, as I

fhall,.

shall, presently, more fully shew. Thus I had once more money.

About this time the French army advanced to within five miles of Magdeburg. This important fortress was, at that time, the key of the whole Prussian power. It required a garrison of sixteen thousand men, and contained not more than fifteen hundred. The French might have marched in unopposed, and at once have put an end to the war. The officers brought me all the news, and my hopes rose as they approached.——What was my astonishment when the major informed me three waggons had entered the town in the night, had been sent back loaded with money, and that the French were retreating! This, I can assure my readers, on my honour, is literally truth, to the eternal disgrace of the French general. The major,

who

who informed me, was himfelf an eye-witnefs of the fact. It was pretended the money was for the army of the King, but every body could guefs whither it was going; it left the town without a convoy, and the French were then in the neighbourhood. Such were the allies of Maria Therefa! The receivers of this money are known in Paris. Not only were my hopes this way fruftrated, but in Ruffia likewife, where the Countefs of Beftuchef, and the chancellor, were fallen into difgrace.

I now imagined another, and indeed a fearful and dangerous, project. The garrifon of Magdeburg, at this moment, confifted but of nine hundred militia, who were difcontented men. Two majors and two lieutenants were in my intereft. The guard of the Star-Fort amounted but to a hundred and fifteen men. Fronting

the

the gate of this fort was the town-gate, guarded only by twelve men and an inferior officer; beside these lay the casemates, in which were seven thousand Croat prisoners. Baron K——y, a captain, and prisoner of war, also was in our interest, and would hold his comrades ready, at a certain place and time, to support my undertaking. Another friend was, under some pretence, to hold his company ready, with their muskets loaded, and the plan was such that I should have had four hundred men in arms, to carry it into execution.

The officer was to have placed the two men we most suspected, and feared, as centinels over me; he was to command them to take away my bed, and, when encumbered, I was to spring out, and shut them in the prison. Clothing and arms were to have been procured, and brought me into my prifon ;

son; the town-gate was to have been surprised; I was to have run to the casemate, and called to the Croats, "Trenck! To arms!" My friends, at the same instant, were to break forth, and the plan was so well concerted that it could not have failed. Magdeburg, the magazine of the army, the royal treasury, arsenal, all would have been mine; and sixteen thousand men, who were then prisoners of war, would have enabled me to keep possession.

The most essential secret, by which all this was to have been effected, I dare not reveal; suffice it to say, every thing was provided for, every thing secure; I shall only add that the garrison, in the harvest months, was exceedingly weakened, because the farmers paid the captains a florin per man each day, and the men, for their labour, likewise, to obtain hands. The fub-governor connived at the practice.

One Lieutenant G—— procured a furlough, to vifit his friends; but, fupplied by me with money, he went to Vienna. I furnifhed him with a letter, addreffed to Counfellors Kempf and Huttner, including a draft for two thoufand ducats; wherein I faid that, by thefe means, I fhould not only foon be at liberty but in poffeffion of the fortrefs of Magdeburg; and that the bearer was intrufted with the reft.

The lieutenant came fafe to Vienna, underwent a thoufand interrogatories, and his name was repeatedly afked. This, fortunately, he concealed. They advifed him not to be concerned in fo dangerous an undertaking; told him I had not fo much money due to me, and gave him, inftead of two thoufand ducats,

one

one thousand florins. With these
he left Vienna, but with very prudent
suspicions, which prevented him ever
more returning to Magdeburg. A
month had scarcely passed before
the late Landgrave of Hesse-Cassel,
then chief governor, entered my prison, shewed me my letter, and demanded to know who had carried the
letter, and who were to free me, and
betray Magdeburg. Whether the
letter was sent immediately to the
king, or the governor, I know not; it
is sufficient that I was once more
betrayed at Vienna. The truth,
was, the administrators of my effects
had acted as if I were deceased, and
chose not to refund two thousand
ducats. They wished not I should
obtain my freedom, in a manner that
would have obliged the government
to reward me, and restore the effects
they had embezzled, and the estates
they

they had feized. What happened afterward in Vienna, which will be related in its place, will inconteftably prove this furmife to be well founded..

Thefe bad men did not, it is true, die in the manner they ought, but they all are dead, and I am ftill living, and like an honeft, though poor, man ; fo did not they die. Be this read, and remembered, by their luxurious heirs,. who refufe to reftore my children to their rights.

My confternation on the appearance of the Landgrave, with my letter in his hand, may well be fuppofed : I had the prefence of mind, however, to deny my hand-writing, and affect aftonifhment at fo crafty a trick. The Landgrave endeavoured to convict me, told me what Lieutenant Kemnitz had repeated at Vienna, concerning my poffeffing

myfelf

myfelf of Magdeburg, and thereby
fhewed me how fully I had been
betrayed. But, as no fuch perfon
exifted as Lieutenant Kemnitz, and
as my friend had fortunately concealed his name, the myftery remained impenetrable, efpecially, as
no one could conceive how a prifoner, in my fituation, could feduce,
or fubdue, the whole garrifon. The
worthy prince left my prifon, apparently fatisfied with my defence;
his heart felt not fatisfaction in the
misfortunes of others.

The next day, a formal examination was taken, at which the fub-
governor Reichmann prefided. I was
accufed as a traitor to my country;
but I obftinately denied my hand-
writing. Proofs, or witneffes, there
were none, and, in anfwer to the principal charge, I faid, " I was no cri-
" minal, but a man calumniated,
" ille-

" illegally imprifoned, and loaded
" with irons; that the King, in the
" year 1746, had cafhiered me, and
" confifcated my parental inheri-
" tance; that, therefore, the laws of
" nature enforced me to feek ho-
" nour, and bread, in a foreign fer-
" vice; and that, finding thefe in
" Auftria, I was become an officer,
" and a faithful fubject of the Em-
" prefs Queen; that I had been, a fe-
" cond time, unoffendingly impri-
" foned; that here I was treated as
" the worft of malefactors, and that
" my only refource was to feek my
" liberty, by fuch means as I could:
" were I, therefore, in this attempt, to
" deftroy the very town of Magde-
" burg, and occafion the lofs of a
" thoufand lives, I fhould ftill be
" guiltlefs. Had I been heard, and
" legally fentenced, previous to my
" imprifonment at Glatz, I fhould
" have

"have been, and have continued, a
"criminal; but not having been
"guilty of any fmall, much lefs of
"any great, crime, equal to my
"punifhment, if fuch crime could
"be, I was, therefore, not account-
"able for confequences: I owed nei-
"ther fidelity, nor duty, to the King
"of Pruffia; for, by the word of
"his power, he had deprived me
"of bread, honour, country, and
"freedom."

Here the examination ended,
without farther difcovery; the officers, however, falling under fufpicion, were all removed, and thus I
loft my beft friends; yet it was not
long before I had gained two
others, which was no difficult matter,
as I knew the national character, and
that none but poor men were made
militia officers. Thus was the governor's precaution fruitlefs, and

every

every body fecretly wifhed I might obtain my freedom.

I fhall never forget the noble manner in which I was treated on this occafion by the Landgrave. This I perfonally acknowledged, fome years afterward, in the city of Caffel, when I heard many things which confirmed all my furmifes concerning Vienna. The Landgrave received me with all grace, favour, and diftinction. I revere his memory, and feek to honour his name. He was the friend of misfortune. When I, not long afterward, fell ill, he fent me his own phyfician, and meat from his table, nor would he fuffer me, during two months, to be waked by the centinels. He, likewife, removed the dreadful collar from my neck; for which he was feverely reprimanded by the King, as he himfelf has fince affured me.

I might

I might fill a volume with incidents attending two other efforts
to efcape, but I will not weary the
reader's patience with too much
repetition. I fhall merely give an
abftract of both.

When I had once more gained
the officers, I made a new attempt
at mining my way out. Not wanting for implements, my chains and
the flooring were foon cut through,
and all was fo carefully replaced I
was under no fear of examination.
I here found my concealed money,
piftols, and other neceffaries, but,
till I had rid myfelf of fome hundred weight of fand, it was impoffible to proceed. For this purpofe I
made two different openings in the
floor: out of the real hole I threw
a great quantity of fand into my
prifon; after which I clofed it with
all poffible care. I then worked

at

at the fecond with fo much noife that I was certain they muft hear me without. About midnight the doors began to thunder, and in they came, detecting me, as I intended they fhould. None of them could conceive why I fhould wifh to break out under the door, where there was a triple guard to pafs. The centinels remained, and, in the morning, prifoners were fent to wheel away the fand. The hole was walled up and boarded, and my fetters were renewed. They laughed at the ridiculoufnefs of my undertaking, but punifhed me by depriving me of my light and bed, which, however, in a fortnight, were both reftored. Of the other hole, out of which moft of the earth had been thrown, no one was aware. The major and lieutenant were too much my friends to remark that they had

removed

removed thrice the quantity of fand the falfe opening could contain. They fuppofed, this ftrange attempt having failed, it would be my laft, and Bruckhaufen grew negligent.

The governor and fub-governor both vifited me, after fome weeks; but, far from the brutality of Borck, the Landgrave fpoke to me with great mildnefs, promifed me his intereft to regain my freedom, when the peace fhould be concluded; told me I had more friends than I might fuppofe, and affured me I had not been quite forgotten by the court of Vienna. The manner in which I anfwered him moved him to the foul in vain he endeavoured to hide his tears, while I, in a moment of exquifite fen-fibility, fell at his feet, rofe, and pleaded like Cicero, happy to have met with a prince, who thought, and felt, like a man.

He promifed me every alleviation, and I gave him my word of honour I would never more attempt to ef- cape, while he remained governor. The manner in which I fpoke en- forced conviction, and it was then that he ordered my neck-collar to be taken off, my window to be un- clofed, my doors every day to be left two hours open, a ftove, which I might light myfelf, to be put in my dungeon, finer linen for my fhirts, and paper to amufe myfelf, by writing down my thoughts. The fheets of paper were to be numbered, when given, and when returned, by the town-major, that I might not abufe this liberty.

Ink was not allowed me, I, there- fore, pricked my finger, fuffered the blood to trickle into a pot, and, when coagulated, warmed it again in my hand, throwing away the

fibrous

fibrous parts, that would not liquefy; by this means, I procured a fuccedaneum for ink, both to write and draw.

I now bufied myfelf with engraving my cups, and verfifying. I had free opportunity to difplay fuch abilities as I poffeffed, to excite efteem, and awaken compaffion. My emulation was increafed, by the knowledge that my productions were feen, and read, at courts, and that the Princefs Amelia, and the Queen herfelf, teftified their fatisfaction. I had foon fubjects fent me ; and the wretch whom the King intended to immure, and bury alive, whofe name no man was to mention, never lived to better purpofe, nor was more famous, than while he vented his groans in this dungeon. My writings produced their effect, and, in reality, regained my freedom. To my cultivation of the fciences, and

 prefence

prefence of mind in danger, am I indebted for all: thefe could not all the
power of Frederic deprive me of; by
thefe I obtained that which he, in his
wrath, and the might of his defpotifm,
had intended to take from me eternally! Yes! this liberty I procured,
though he had continually anfwered
all petitions in my behalf—" He is
" a dangerous man; and, fo long as I
" have life, he fhall never fee the
" light!" Yet have I feen it, as broadly
as himfelf, during his life: after his
death, I have feen it without reveng-
ing myfelf, otherwife than by prov-
ing my innocence, and virtue, to a
monarch, who oppreffed becaufe he
knew me not, becaufe he would not
recal the hafty fentence of anger,
or own it was *poffible* he might be
miftaken. No! In my writings I
have fought only to appeafe him, to
juftify, and prove, the *greatnefs* of

his

his foul! He died convinced of my integrity, yet, without affording me retribution! Perhaps, he recollected my fufferings, and knew retribution was impoffible. Enough! If fo it can be, peace be to his afhes! Man is formed by misfortune; virtue is active in adverfity. Perhaps, had I lived in uninterrupted happinefs, pofterity would have heard little of my name. It is indifferent to me, that the companions of my youth have their ears gratified, delighted, with the titles of General! Field-Marfhal! I have learned to live without fuch additions. I am known in my works. Hence, has it often been afked, why is not he, alfo, a minifter, or a General. Bleffed Content! Thee have I learned to tafte, unalloyed by pride! Repofe, thrice bleffed! Thee do I enjoy, in the haven of the wife, after ftorms

I 3

and

and horrors paft !—May my hiftory, my example, confole the afflicted, ftrike terror to the guilty, bridle youth's impetuofity, and infpire the fuffering with fortitude !

I return to my dungeon. Here, after my laft conference with the Landgrave, I waited my coming fate, with a mind more at eafe than that of many a prince in his palace. My dawn of hope, daily, grew more bright. The newfpapers, they brought me, foretold approaching peace, on which all my dependance was placed, and I paffed eighteen months calmly, and without further attempt.

The father of the Landgrave died ; he had, till then, been only heredi-tary prince ; and Magdeburg now loft its noble governor. The wor-thy Reichmann, however, teftified for me all compaffion and efteem ; I

had

had books, my time was employed, and, therefore, ſtole, unperceived, away. Impriſonment, and chains, to me, were become habitual, and freedom, in all her lovely forms, ſleeping, and awake, in hope approached.

About this time, I wrote the poems, found in my works, called, the Macedonian Hero; The Dream Realized; and the Fables contained in the firſt volume, moſt of which have reference to myſelf. The moſt, and the beſt, of my poems, are now loſt to me. The mind's ſenſibility, when the body is impriſoned, is ſtrongly rouzed, nor can all the aids of the library equal this advantage. Perhaps, I may recover ſome of them in Berlin: if ſo, the world may learn what my thoughts then were. When I was ſet at liberty, I had none but ſuch as I remembered, and theſe I committed to writing.

On

On my firſt perſonal viſit to the Landgrave of Heſſe-Caſſel, I received a volume of them, written in my own blood; but there were certainly eight of theſe, which I ſhall ſcarcely ever regain.

The death of Elizabeth, the depoſing of Peter III. and the acceſſion of Catherine II. produced peace. On the receipt of this intelligence, I endeavoured to provide for all poſſible contingencies. The worthy Captain K— had opened me a correſpondence with Vienna; I was aſſured of ſupport; but was, likewiſe, aſſured the adminiſtrators, and thoſe who poſſeſſed my eſtates, would throw every poſſible impediment in the way of freedom. I endeavoured to perſuade another officer to aid my eſcape, but in vain: no ſecond Schell was to be found.

The

The will confented, but the heart recoiled.

I, therefore, opened my old hole, and my friends affifted me, all in their power, further to difembarrafs myfelf of fand. My money melted away, but they provided me with tools, gunpowder, and a good fword. I had remained fo long quiet that my flooring was no more examined.

My intent was to wait the peace, and, fhould I ftill continue in chains, then would I have my fubterranean paffage to the rampart ready for efcape. For my further fecurity, an old lieutenant had, with my money, purchafed a houfe in the fuburbs, where I might lie concealed. Gummern, in Saxony, is two miles from Magdeburg: here a friend, with two good horfes, was to wait a whole year, to ride on the glacis of Klofterbergen, on the firft, and

fifteenth

fifteenth, of each month, and, at a given fignal, to haften to my affift-ance.

My paffage was to be ready in cafe of emergency ; I, therefore, re-moved the upper planking, broke up the two under-beds, cut the boards into chips, and burnt them in my ftove. By this I obtained fo much additional room as to pro-ceed half way with my mine. Li-nen again was brought me, fand-bags made, and thus I fuccefsfully proceeded to all but the laft opera-tion. Every thing was afterward fo well clofed, and concealed, that I had nothing to fear, from the nar-roweft infpection, fufficient of the under flooring being left to fupport the upper, and it appeared doubly nailed, as before, to avoid fufpicion, efpecially as the new come garrifon

could

could not know what was the original length of the planks.

This fevere labour reduced me again to a very feeble ftate of body; and, by the return of the regulars, I, in a moment, was deprived of all my friends.

I muft, in this place, relate a dreadful accident, which I cannot, even now, remember, without fhuddering, and the terror of which has often haunted my very dreams.

While mining under the foundation of the rampart, juft as I was going to carry out the fand-bag, I ftruck my foot againft a ftone in the wall above, which fell down and clofed up the paffage.

What was my horror, to find myfelf thus buried alive! After a fhort time for reflection, I began to work the fand away from the fide, that I might obtain room to turn round.

16   By

By good fortune, there were some feet of empty space, into which I threw the sand as I worked it away; but the small quantity of air soon made it so foul that I, a thousand times, wished myself dead, and made several attempts to strangle myself. Further labour began to seem impossible. Thirst almost deprived me of my senses, but, as often as I put my mouth to the sand, I inhaled fresh air. My sufferings were incredible, and, I imagine, I passed full eight hours in this distraction of horror. Of all dreadful deaths, surely, such a death as this is the most dreadful. My spirits fainted; again I somewhat recovered, again I began to labour, but the earth was as high as my chin, and I had no more space, into which I might throw the sand, that I might turn round. I made a more desperate effort, drew

my

my body into a ball, and turned round; I now faced the ftone, which was as wide as the whole paffage, but, there being an opening at the top, I refpired frefher air. My next labour was to root away the fand under the ftone, and let it fink, fo that I might creep over, and, by this means, at length, I once more happily arrived in my dungeon!

The morning was advanced; I fat myfelf down fo exhaufted that I fuppofed it was impoffible I had time, or ftrength, to cover up and conceal my hole. After half an hour's reft, however, my fortitude returned: again I went to work, and, fcarcely had I ended, before the refounding locks and bolts told the approach of my vifitors.

They found me pale as death: I complained of the head-ach, and continued fome days fo much affected,

ed, by the fatigue I had fuftained, that I began to imagine my lungs were impaired. After a time, health and ftrength returned, but, perhaps, of all my nights of horror, this was the moft horrible. I long repeatedly dreamed I was buried alive in the center of the earth ; and now, though three and twenty years are elapfed, my fleep is ftill haunted by this vifion.

After this accident, whenever I worked in my cavity, I hung a knife round my neck, that, in cafe I fhould be again fo inclofed, I might fhorten my miferies. Over the ftone that had fallen were feveral others that hung tottering, under which I was,, feveral hundred times, obliged to creep. Nothing could deter me from endeavouring to obtain my liberty !

When

When my paſſage was ready, ſo that I could break out when I pleaſed, I wrote various letters to my friends at Vienna, and alſo an impaſſioned memorial to my ſovereign. When the militia left Magdeburg, and the regulars returned, I took an affecting leave of my friends, who had behaved to me with ſo much humanity, and ſo benevolently ſupplied my wants. — Several weeks elapſed before they departed, and I learnt that General Riedt was appointed ambaſſador from Vienna to Berlin.

I had ſeen the world; I knew this general was not averſe to a bribe; I wrote him a moving letter, conjuring him not to abandon me, and to act with perhaps more ardour in my behalf than his inſtructions might imply. I incloſed a draft, for ſix thouſand florins, on my effects at

Vienna,

Vienna, and he received four thousand more from one of my relations.
I have to thank these ten thousand
florins for my freedom, which I obtained nine months after. My vouchers shew the six thousand florins were
paid in April '1763, to the order
of General Riedt. The other four
thousand I thankfully repaid, when
at liberty, to my friend.

I received intelligence, before the
garrison departed, that no stipulation
had been made, on my behalf, at the
peace of Hubertsberg.*   The Vienna plenipotentiaries, after, and not
before, the articles were signed, men-

* The release of Trenck was so feebly mentioned, by the Austrian plenipotentiary, that
Hertzberg, the Prussian minister, took not the
least notice of the affair.   T.

See Fischer Geschichte Fried. II.
Theil II. S. 246.

tioned

tioned my name to Hertzberg, but with little earneftnefs of folicitation. From Berlin, indeed, I received private affurances of every effort being made to move Frederic, a promife on which I could much better rely than on my protectors at Vienna, who fo many years had left me in misfortune. I, therefore, determined to wait three months longer, and, fhould I ftill find myfelf neglected, to owe my efcape to myfelf.

On the change of the garrifon, the officers, being all of the nobility, were much more difficult to gain than the former. The majors literally obeyed their orders ; their help was unneceffary ; but ftill I fighed for my old friends. I had only ammunition bread again for food, as no one fupplied me with the leaft comfortable addition.

My

My time hung very heavy; every thing was carefully examined on the change of the garrison. A still stricter scrutiny might occur, and all my projects be discovered. This had nearly been effected by accident, as I shall here relate. I had, two years before, so tamed a mouse that it would play round me, and eat from my mouth: in this small animal I discovered proofs of intelligence too great to easily gain belief: were I to write them, priests would rail, monks grumble, and such philosophers as suppose man alone endowed with the power of thought, allowing nothing, but what they call instinct, to animals, would proclaim me a fabulous writer, and my opinions heterodox to what they suppose found philosophy. Should I live, perhaps, I may hereafter publish an essay on this subject, in which, this my mouse,

and

and a spider, will appear as remarkable characters.

This intelligent mouse had nearly been my ruin. I had diverted myself with it during the night; it had been nibbling at my door, and capering on a trencher. The centinels happened to hear our amusement, called the officers; they heard also, and added all was not right in my dungeon. At day-break, my doors resounded; the town-major, a smith, and mason entered: strict search was begun; flooring, walls, chains, and my own person, were all scrutinized, but in vain. They asked what was the noise they had heard: I mentioned the mouse, whistled, and it came and jumped upon my shoulder. Orders were given I should be deprived of its society; I earnestly intreated they would at least spare its life. The officer on guard gave me

his

his word of honour, he would prefent it to a lady, who would treat it
with the utmoft tendernefs.

He took it away, turned it loofe in
the guard-room, but it was tame to
me alone, and fought a hiding place.
It had fled to my prifon door, and,
at the hour of vifitation, ran into
my dungeon, immediately teftifying
its joy by its antic leaping between
my legs. It is worthy remark that
it had been taken away blindfold,
that is to fay, wrapped in a hand-
kerchief. The guard-room was a
hundred paces from my dungeon.
How then did it find its mafter?
Did it know, or did it wait for, the
hour of vifitation? Had it remarked
the doors were daily opened?

All were defirous of obtaining
this moufe, but the major carried
it off for his lady; fhe put it into a
cage, where it pined, refufed all
fufte-

uftenance, and, in a few days, was
ound dead.

The lofs of this little companion
nade me, for fome time, quite melancholy, yet, on the laft examination,
. perceived it had fo eaten away the
bread, by which I had concealed the
crevices I had made in cutting the
loor, that the examiners muft be
ll but blind not to difcover them.

was convinced my faithful little
riend had fallen a neceffary victim
o its mafter's fafety. My keepers
were perfuaded I had neither the
will nor the power to make further
ttempts at freedom. This accident,
owever, determined me not to wait
ven the three months.

I have already related horfes
ere to be kept ready, on the firft
nd fifteenth, and I only fuffered the
rft of Auguft to pafs, becaufe I
ould not injure the worthy Major
Pfuhl,

Pfuhl, who had treated me with more compaffion than his comrades, and whofe day of vifitation it was. On the fifteenth I determined to fly. This refolution formed, I waited in anxious expectation of the day when a new, and again moft·remarkable fucceffion of accidents happened.

An alarm of fire had obliged the major of the day to repair in hafte to the town; he, therefore, committed the keys to the lieutenant. The latter, coming to vifit me, with a look of compaffion, afked —— " Dear " Trenck, have you never, during " feven years that you have been un- " der the guard of the militia, found " a man like Schell ?"—" Alas! fir," anfwered I, " fuch friends are indeed " rare; the will of many has been " good: each knew I could make his " fortune, but none had courage " enough for fo defperate an attempt!

" Money

(191)

" Money I have diftributed freely,
" but have received little help."

" Money ! how do you obtain mo-
" ney in this dungeon ?"—" From a
" fecret correfpondent at Vienna, by
" whom I am ftill fupplied. If I can
" ferve you, command me : I will do
" it willingly, without afking any re-
" turn." So faying, I immediately
took fifty ducats from between the
pannels, and gave them to the lieutenant. At firft he refufed, but, at
length, accepted them with fear.—
He left me, promifed to return, pretended to fhut the door, and kept
his word. He now avowed debt
obliged him to defert, that this had
long been his determination, and that,
could he affift me, at the fame time,
he was ready and willing. I had only
to fhew how this might be effected.

We continued two hours in conference ; a plan was foon formed,

ap-

approved, and almoſt a certainty of ſucceſs demonſtrated; eſpecially, when I told him I had two horſes in waiting. We vowed eternal friendſhip, I gave him fifty additional ducats, and he had never before been ſo rich; his whole debts, which would oblige him to deſert, not amounting to more than two hundred rix-dollars, which, however, he never could have diſcharged out of his pay.

He was to prepare four keys, that were to reſemble thoſe of my dungeon; the latter were to be exchanged on the day of flight, being kept in the guard-room while the major was with General Walrabe. He was to give the grenadiers on guard leave of abſence for ſome hours, or ſend them into the town on various pretences. The centinels at the gate he was to call from their duty, and

thoſe

thofe placed over me were to be fent into my dungeon, to take away my bed; while encumbered with this, I was to fpring out, and lock them in, after which we were to mount our horfes, kept ready, and ride full fpeed to Gummern. Every thing was to be prepared within a week, when he was again to mount guard. We had fcarcely fully formed our project before the centinels called, the major was coming; he, accordingly, haftily barred up the doors, and the major paffed to General Walrabe.

No man now was happier than myfelf, in a dungeon though I was: my hopes of efcape were triple; the mediation at Berlin, the mine I had made, and my new friend, the lieutenant.

Intoxicated with hope and joy, then, when moft my mind ought to

have been cool and clear, I seemed
to have loſt my underſtanding. I
came to a reſolution which will appear, to every reaſonable man, ex-
travagant, abſurd, and pitiable. I
was vain enough, ſtupid enough,
mad enough, to form the deſign of
caſting myſelf on the generoſity and
magnanimity of the *Great Frederic!*—
Should this fail, I ſtill thought my
lieutenant a certain ſaviour.

Having heated my imagination
with this lamentable ſcheme, I expected the hour of viſitation with
anxiety. The major entered; I be-
ſpoke him thus:

" I know ſir, the great Prince
" Ferdinand is again in Magdeburg."
(My new friend had told me this.)
" Be pleaſed to infoim him that he
" may firſt examine my priſon, dou-
" ble the centinels, and afterward
" give me his commands, ſtating at
 " what

"what hour it will pleafe him I
"fhould make my appearance, in
"perfect freedom, on the glacis of
"Klofterbergen. If I prove myfelf
"capable of this, I then hope for
"the protection of Prince Ferdi-
"nand; and that he will relate my
"proceeding to the King, who may
"thereby be convinced of my inno-
"cence, and the perfect clearnefs of
"my confcience."

The major was aftonifhed; fuppofed my brain turned. The propofal he held to be ridiculous, and
the performance impoffible. I, however, perfifted; he rode to town, and
returned with the fub-governor,
Reichmann; the town-major, Riding;
and the major of infpection. The
anfwer they delivered was—That the
Prince promifed me his protection,
the King's favour, and a certain releafe from my chains, fhould I prove

the truth of my affertion. I required they would appoint a time;
they ridiculed the thing as impoffible, and, at laft, faid that it would
be fufficient could I only prove the
practicability of fuch a fcheme;
but, fhould I refufe, they would
immediately break up the whole
flooring, and place centinels in my
dungeon night and day; adding,
the governor would not admit of
any actual breaking out.

After the moft folemn promifes
of good faith, I immediately difencumbered myfelf of my chains, raifed
up my flooring, gave them my arms
and implements, and alfo two keys,
that my friends had procured me, to
the doors of the fubterranean gallery.
This gallery I defired them to enter,
and found, with their fword-hilts,
at the place through which I was to
break, which might be done in a

few

few minutes. I further deſcribed
the road I was to take through the
gallery, informed them that two of
the doors had not been ſhut for ſix
months, and to the others they already had the keys; adding, I had
horſes ready at the glacis, that would
be immediately ready; the ſtables
for which were unknown to them.

They went, examined, returned,
put queſtions, which I anſwered
with as much preciſion as the engi-
neer could have done who built the
Star-Fort. They left me with ſeem-
ing friendſhip, continued away about
an hour, came back, told me the
prince was aſtoniſhed at what he had
heard, that he wiſhed me all happineſs, and then took me, unfettered,
to the guard-houſe. The major
came in the evening, treated us
with a ſumptuous ſupper, aſſured
me every thing would happen to

my

my wishes, and that Prince Ferdinand had already written to Berlin.

The guard was reinforced next day: two grenadiers entered the officer's room as centinels. The whole guard loaded with ball before my eyes, the draw-bridges were raised in open day, and precautions were taken as if it were supposed I intended to make attempts as desperate as those I had made at Glatz.

I now saw numerous workmen employed on my dungeon, and carts bringing quarry-stones. The officers on guard behaved with great kindness, kept a good table, at which I ate, but two centinels, and an under officer, never quitted the guard-room. Conversation was very cautious, and this continued five or six days: at length, it was my new friend, the lieutenant's, turn to mount guard; he appeared to be as

friendly

friendly as formerly, but conference
was difficult: he, however, found
an opportunity to exprefs his aftonifhment at my ill-timed difcovery,
told me the prince knew nothing of
the affair, and that the report propagated through the garrifon was, I
had been furprifed in making a new
attempt.

I now faw my error, but, alas!
too late. I affured my friend this
ftep had been occafioned by my
reliance on his promife. He lamented my miftake, but affirmed
himfelf ftill the fame. My courage
ftrengthened, and I vowed vengeance againft the mean conduct of
the fub-governor.

My dungeon was completed in
about a week. The town-major
and major of the day re-conducted
me to it. My foot only was chained
to the wall, but with links twice as

K 4

ftrong

ſtrong as formerly; the remainder of my irons were never after added.

Inſtead of flooring, the dungeon was paved with huge flag ſtones. The priſon was made impenetrable. That part of my money only was ſaved which I had concealed in the pannels of the door, and the chimney of the ſtove; ſome thirty louis-d'ors, hidden about my clothes, were taken from me.

While the ſmith was rivetting my chains, I addreſſed myſelf to the ſub-governor. " Is this the conſe-" quence of the pledged honour of " the Prince? Has the magnani-" mity of my conduct deſerved ſuch " treatment? But think not you " deceive me, I am acquainted with " the falſe reports that have been " ſpread; the truth will ſoon come " to light, and the unworthy be put " to ſhame. Nay, I now foretell " you,

" you, Trenck fhall not be much
" longer in your power; for, were
" you to build your dungeon of
" fteel, it would ftill be infufficient
" to contain me."

They fmiled at my threats.
Reichmann, however, defired me to
take courage, and faid I might, probably, foon obtain my freedom after
a proper manner. My firm reliance
on my friend, the lieutenant, gave
me, inftead of appearing funken and
defpondent, a degree of confidence
that amazed them all.

It is here neceffary farther to explain this affair. When I had obtained my liberty, I vifited Prince
Ferdinand, at Brunfwic. He informed
me the majors had not made a true
report, being afraid of reprimand
for their own careleffnefs. Their
ftory was, they had caught me at
work, and, had it not been for their

K 5   extreme

extreme diligence, I fhould, certainly, have made my efcape. Prince Ferdinand heard the truth fome time after, and informed the King, who, from that time, only waited a favourable opportunity to reftore me to liberty.

Such is the way of the world! Such the manner in which the moft generous, the moft noble, acts are often painted! I was, in this cafe, the filly facrifice of my own vanity. Thofe who guarded me were afhamed of their neglect, and, to avoid reprimand, which would not effectually have injured any of them, was I again led to my flaughter-houfe. Such has been the iffue, through life, of many noble undertakings; where others have taken advantage of my too great opennefs of heart, and procured reward to themfelves by my labours.

Once

Once more was I immured, curf-ing in my heart the cruelties of kings and governors: this time, however, they were innocent, be-caufe deceived.

I waited in anxious hope for the day when my deliverer was to mount guard. What again was my defpair when, inftead of him, I faw ano-ther lieutenant. I buoyed myfelf up with the expectation that acci-dent was the occafion of this, but I remained three weeks in the fame fufpence, and faw him no more. Afk I durft not, but heard, at length, he had left the corps of grenadiers, and, therefore, was no longer to mount guard at the Star-Fort. Whether he was afraid, repented his engagement, or that the hundred ducats had procured him better profpects, I neither know, nor ever wifh to know. Should he ever read

this

this book, and fhould he really have deceived me, let him alfo read that he has my hearty forgivenefs, and that I applaud myfelf for never having faid any thing by which he might be injured. Others, perhaps, being thus deferted by him in misfortune, after fo many proteftations, and condefcending to receive money, would have been more revengeful. He might, having paid his debts, repent his promife; he might have trufted another friend with the enterprife, and have been himfelf betrayed: but, be it as it may, his abfence cut off all hope.

I bitterly now repented my folly and untimely vanity: melancholy feized my mind; I had brought my misfortunes on myfelf. When I had removed every impediment, the confidence I placed in the honour of man again plunged me near fix

months

months longer in affliction, doubled by defpair. I had myfelf rendered my dungeon impenetrable. Death would have followed but for the dependence I placed in the court of Vienna.

The officers foon remarked the lofs of my accuftomed fortitude, and gloomy thoughtfulnefs. I was lefs induftrious on my cups; the verfes I wrote were defponding. The only comfort they could give was, " Pa- " tience, dear Trenck; your condi- " tion cannot be worfe; the King " may not live for ever." Small confolation this. Were I fick, they told me I then might hope my fufferings would foon have an end. If I recovered, they pitied me, and lamented their continuance. What man of my rank and expectations ever endured what I have endured,

ever

ever was treated as I have been treated !

Peace had been concluded nine months. I was forgotten. At laft, however, when I fuppofed all hope loft, the 24th of December, and the day of freedom, came! At the hour of parade Count Schlieben, lieutenant of the guards, arrived, and brought orders for my releafe !

The fub-governor fuppofed me weaker in intellect than I really was, and would not too fuddenly tell me thefe happy tidings. He knew not the prefence of mind, the fortitude, which the various dangers I had feen had made habitual. Self-praife offends; yet never was I too much elated in profperity, depreffed in adverfity; never timid or undetermined in the moment of danger; and, for the truth of this, I appeal to all who have known me perfonally,

ally, or been acquainted with thofe who have feen me in fuch fituations.

My doors, for the LAST TIME, refounded! Several people entered; their countenances were more than ufually cheerful, and the fub-governor at their head, at length, faid, " This time, my dear Trenck, I am " the joyful meffenger of good news. " Prince Ferdinand has prevailed on " the King to let your irons be " taken off."——Accordingly, to work went the fmith——" You " fhall, alfo," continued he, " have " a better apartment." " I am free " then," faid I, " and you are afraid " to tell me fo too fuddenly. Speak! " fear not! I can moderate my " tranfports."

" Then you are free!" was the reply.

The fub-governor firft embraced me, and afterward his attendants.

He

He afked me what clothes I would wifh. I anfwered the uniform of my regiment. The taylor attended, and took meafure. Reichmann told him it muft be made by the morning. The man excufed himfelf, becaufe it was Chriftmas eve——" So " then this gentleman muft remain in " his dungeon, becaufe it is holiday " with you." The taylor was anfwered, and promifed to be ready.

The fmith having ended his work, I was taken to the guard-room: congratulations were univerfal, and the town-major adminiftered the oath cuftomary to all ftate prifoners.

1ft. That I fhould avenge myfelf on no man.

2ndly. That I fhould neither enter the Pruffian nor Saxon ftates.

3dly. That I fhould never relate, by fpeech, or in writing, what had happened to me.

4thly.

4thly. And that, fo long as the King lived, I fhould neither ferve in a civil nor military capacity.

Count Schlieben delivered me a letter from the imperial minifter, General Riedt, in Berlin, to the following purport: that he was heartily rejoiced at having found an opportunity of obtaining my liberty from the King; that I muft cheerfully obey the requifitions of Count Schlieben, whofe orders were to accompany me to Prague.

e " Yes, dear Trenck," faid Schlieben, " I am to conduct you in a " covered waggon through Drefden " to Prague, with orders not to " fuffer you to fpeak to any one on " the road. I have received three " hundred ducats from General " Riedt, to defray the expence of " travelling. A waggon muft be " purchafed; but, as all things cannot

" be

" be prepared to-day, the sub-go-
" vernor has determined we shall
" depart to-morrow night."

Having joyfully acquiesced, Count
Schlieben remained with me; the
others, after a short conversation,
returned to the town, and I dined, in
company with the major of the day and
the officers on guard, with General
Walrabe in his prison. Here this
gentleman died, in 1774, having remained at Magdeburg eight and
twenty years. His confinement,
however, was both deserved and
rendered supportable.

Once more at liberty, I walked
about the fortifications, to accustom
myself to light and air, and collected
the money I had concealed in my
dungeon, which amounted to about
seventy ducats. To every man on
guard I gave a ducat, to the centinels then on duty over me each
three,

three, and ten ducats to be divided
among the relief-guard. I fent the
officer on guard a prefent from
Prague, and the remainder of my
money I beftowed on the widow of
the kind, the honeft, the worthy
Gefhardt. He, poor fellow, was no
more, and fhe had entrufted the
fecret of the thoufand florins to a
young foldier, who, fpending too
freely, was fufpected, betrayed her,
and fhe paffed two years in the
houfe of correction. Gefhardt never received any punifhment; he
was in the field. Had he left any
children, I fhould, in duty, have
provided for them. To the widow
of the man who hung himfelf before
my prifon door, in the year 1756, I
gave thirty ducats, lent me by
Schlieben.

The night was riotous, the guard
made merry, and I paffed moft of

it

it in their company. I was vifited
by all the generals of the garrifon
on Chriftmas morning, for I was
not allowed to enter the town.
Boots, uniform, all were ready by
noon. I was dreffed, viewed myfelf
in the glafs, and found pleafure; but
the tumult of my own paffions, the
congratulations I received, and the
vivacity of every thing round me,
prevented my remembering incidents minutely.

How much room for reflection
did this fcene afford! My intrinfic
worth then and twenty-four hours
before, when in prifon, was the
fame; yet, how wonderful an altera-
tion in the carriage and countenance
of thofe by whom I had been fo
ftrictly guarded! I was treated with
friendfhip, diftinction, attention, and
flattery. And why? Becaufe thofe
fetters had dropt off which I had

never

never juſtly borne. Oh World! what art thou? What, indeed, in deſpotic ſtates! What is merit, what virtue, where arbitrary power diſpoſes of the fate of men?

Evening came, and with it Count Schlieben, a waggon, and four poſt-horſes. After a very affecting fare-well, we departed. Who could have perſuaded me I ſhould have ſhed tears at leaving Magdeburg? Yet tears I actually did ſhed. It ſeems equally ſtrange that I lived here ten years, yet never ſaw the town.

I ſhall not weary the reader's patience with the trivial incidents of our journey. The exact duration of my impriſonment at Magdeburg was nine years, five months, and ſome days; add to theſe the ſeven-teen months impriſonment at Glatz, and the amount is eleven years. Thus did the prime of life, the

brighteſt

brighteft hours in the day of man, pafs in imprifonment. Thus was I robbed of time, which monarchs have not the power to reftore ; thus, too, was my body weakened, thus my health impaired, fo that now in my decline of life, a fecond time, I fuffer in the gloom, the damp, and the chains, of the dungeon of Magdeburg.

The reader would now hope, having obtained my freedom, that my calamities were all at an end; yet do I declare, upon my honour, I would prefer the fufferings of the Star-Fort, to thofe I have fince endured in Auftria, efpecially the laft fix years, while Krügel, and Zetto, were my referendaries, and curators.

It may happen that I may publifh a third volume, * in which I may more

* This third volume the Baron has publifhed.

more openly, and fully, relate the misfortunes of two and twenty years, particularly the laft fix, fpent at Vienna. At this moment, I am obliged to be guarded in my expreffions. I have, already, put my enemies to fhame; but the hope of juftice, or reward, on this fide the grave, is vain. No rewards are beftowed on him, who, with all the confcioufnefs of integrity, demands, and does not implore. The facts, I fhall relate, will, indeed, feem improbable, nay incredible, yet have I, in my own hands, the indifputable vouchers of their verity. I repeat the words of my preface:

" If

ed. It is the third volume of the prefent tranflation; but it is neceffary to preferve this, and fimilar paffages, becaufe they contain circumftances by which fufpenfe is kept alive.

T.

" If my right hand is guilty of
" writing untruths, in this book,
" may the common executioner fever
" it from my body, and, in the me-
" mory of posterity, may I live a
" villain."

Having thus called the reader's
attention to its truth, I proceed with
my hiftory.

On the 2d of January, I arrived,
with Count Schlieben, fafely at
Prague, and, the fame day, he delivered me to the then governor, the
duke of Deuxponts. He received
me with kindnefs, and diftinction;
we dined with him two fucceffive
days, and all Prague was anxious
to fee a man who had furmounted
ten years of fufferings, fo unheard-
of as mine. Here I received three
thoufand florins, and paid General
Riedt his three hundred ducats,
which he had advanced Count
Schlieben,

Schlieben, for the expences of my journey, the repayment of which he demanded, in his letter, although he had already received ten thoufand florins. The expence of returning I alfo paid to Schlieben, made him a prefent, and provided myfelf with fome neceffaries. After remaining a few days at Prague, a courier arrived from Vienna, to whom, it is moft worthy of remark, I was obliged to pay forty florins, with an order from government to bring me, under a ftrong guard, from Prague to Vienna. My fword was demanded; Captain Count Wela, and two inferior officers, entered the carriage, which I was obliged to purchafe, in company with me, and brought me to Vienna. I took up a thoufand florins more, in Prague, to defray thefe expences, and was obliged, in

Vienna, to pay the captain fifty ducats, for travelling charges back.

At treatment like this, what were the fenfations of my foul! I ought to have re-entered Vienna, in triumph, like the martyr of his country, haftening to receive his reward; I, on the contrary, was brought back like a criminal, was fent, as a prifoner, to the barracks, there kept in the chamber of Lieutenant Blonket, with orders that I fhould be fuffered to write to no one, fpeak to no one, without a ticket, from the counfellors Kempf or Huttner. Thefe good gentlemen, during my imprifonment, had been the adminiftrators of my effects!

So I remained fix weeks: at length, the colonel of the regiment of Poniatowfky, the prefent fieldmarfhal, Count Alton, fpoke to me. I related what I fuppofed were the

reafons

reafons of my being thus kept a prifoner in Vienna; and to the exertions of this worthy man am I indebted that the abominable intentions of my enemies were fruſtrated, which were to have me imprifoned, during life, as infane, in the fortrefs of Gratz. Had they once removed me from Vienna, all had been loſt, and I ſhould, certainly, have pined away the poor remainder of my life, in a madhoufe. Yet, when at liberty, could I never obtain juſtice againſt thefe men! By their means, was the Emprefs perfuaded that my brain was affected, and that I, continually, uttered the moſt violent threats againſt the King of Pruſſia. The election of a king of the Romans was then in agitation, and the court was apprehenfive left I, with a raſh defire of vengeance, ſhould act fomething, that might offend the Pruſſian envoy. General Riedt had, moreover, been obliged to promife Frederic that I fhould not be fuffered to appear in Vienna, and that they fhould hold a moft wary eye over me. The Emprefs-Queen felt compaffion for my fuppofed difeafe, and afked if no affiftance could be afforded me; to which they anfwered, I had feveral times been let blood, but that I ftill remained a very dangerous man. They added that I fquandered my money ftrangely, having taken up, and difperfed, four thoufand florins in fix days, at Prague; that it would, therefore, be proper to appoint curators, or guardians, to impede fuch extravagancies. Thus do the wicked utter their falfehoods! Thus do they cloud, and obfcure, the throne, making truth invifible!

Count Alton, however, fpoke of
me,

me, and my hard deſtiny, to the Counteſs Paar, miſtreſs of the ceremonies to the Empreſs-Queen, a noble-minded lady. The late Emperor entered the chamber, while I was the ſubject of diſcourſe, and aſked whether I never had any lucid intervals. "May it pleaſe your "majeſty," anſwered Alton, "he has "now been ſeven weeks, in cuſtody, "at my barracks, and I never in my "life met a more reaſonable, or "more agreeable man. There muſt "be ſomething myſterious in this "affair, or he could not be treated "as a madman, or ſo repreſented at "court. That he is not ſo, in any- "wiſe, I pledge my honour."

The next day, the Emperor ſent Count Thurn, grand maſter of the Arch-Duke Leopold, to ſpeak to me. In him I found a worthy man, an enlightened philoſopher, and a lover of

his

his country. To him I related how I had twice been betrayed, twice fold at Vienna, during my imprifonment; demonftrated that my adminiftrators had only acted in this vile manner that I might be imprifoned for life, and they remain undifturbed in poffeffion of my effects. We converfed together two hours, during which many things were faid, that prudence will not permit me, here, to repeat. I gained his confidence, and his heart, and he continued my friend till death. He left me, promifed protection, returned the following day, and procured me an audience of the Emperor.

I fpoke with freedom; the audience lafted more than an hour. At length the Emperor was fo moved that he rofe from his feat, and retired into the next apartment; I faw

the

the tears drop from his eyes. With sympathetic enthusiasm, I fell at his feet, embraced his knees, and wished for the presence of a Rubens, or Apelles, to preserve a scene so highly honourable to the memory of the monarch, and paint the sensations of an innocent man, imploring the protection of a great, a just, and a compassionate prince. I feel myself unequal to do his memory that justice it deserves. Words I had none, but my looks, my tears, were indeed eloquent.————The Emperor tore himself from me, and I departed, with sensations, such as only those can know who, themselves being virtuous, have, unfortunately, met with vile and wicked men.

The ill-judging world has called the Emperor Francis a weak Prince. To me he seems superior

to

to Cæsar, or *Frederic the Great.* That
he had a noble mind, what I have
cited is an irrefragable proof; and,
had not death robbed me of his protection, then, when he found me
worthy, I fhould long fince have regained the Hungarian eftates I have
now for ever loft.

I returned to my barracks in all
the raptures of joy, and an order,
the next day, came for my releafe. I
went, with Count Alton, to the Countefs Paar, who defired to fee me, and,
by her mediation, I obtained a private audience of the Emprefs.

I cannot defcribe the kindnefs of
the fovereign; how much fhe pitied
my fufferings, how much fhe admired my fortitude. I had not opportunity to fpeak a word; her pro-
feffions of pity preventing my ftating
the juftnefs of my cafe. She told
me fhe was informed of all the vile
arti-

artifices practifed againft me in Vienna : required, however, I fhould mention no paft grievances, fhould forgive all my enemies, avoid all retrofpect, and pafs all the accounts of my adminiftrators. —— I would have fpoken. —— " Do not com-
" plain of any thing," faid fhe, " but
" act as I defire — I know all—you
" fhall be recompenfed by me ;
" you deferve reward and repofe, and
" thefe you fhall enjoy." —— What could I do ? — I muft either fign, whatever was given me to fign, or be fent to a madhoufe. I received orders to accompany M. Piftrich to Counfellor Ziegler : thither I went, and the next day was obliged to fign, in their prefence, the following conditions:

First—That I acknowledged the will of Trenck to be valid.

L 5

Second-

Secondly — That I renounced all claim to the Sclavonian estates, relying alone on her Majesty's favour.

Thirdly—That I solemnly acquitted my accountants and curators: And,

Lastly—That I would not continue in Vienna.

What more could have been asked of me, had I, instead of reward, deserved punishment?

This I must sign, or languish in a prison. If such be not arbitrary power, what is?

So was I dealt with! The Empress was prevented acting greatly and nobly.—It is an eternal truth that this my mistreatment was occasioned by my refusing to hear mass; and that the possessors of my estates were under the protection of the Jesuits.*

* The confessor of the Empress was a Jesuit.   T.

What

What did I feel! How did my blood boil while I figned! The confidence I had in myfelf affured me I could obtain honourable employment in any country of Europe, by the exertion of my talents, the labours of my mind, and the faithful recital of all my woes. At that time I had no children; I, therefore, little regretted what I had loft, or the poor portion that remained.

Juftly diffatisfied, I determined to avoid Auftria eternally. My honeft pride would never fuffer me, by clandeftine and infidious arts, to approach the throne. I knew no fuch mode of foliciting for juftice, hence was I an unequal match for my enemies; hence my ills, hence my misfortunes. Complaints, and appeals to juftice, were artfully reprefented as the fplenetic effufions of a man never to be fatisfied. By courts of

juftice

juſtice I had been plundered; appeals to them were, therefore, vain indeed.

My too ſenſible heart was preyed upon, and corroded, by the treatment I met at Vienna. I, who, with ſo much fortitude, ſuch unſhaken honour, had ſuffered ſo much in the cauſe of Vienna, on whom the eyes of all Germany were at this time fixed, to ſee what ſhould be the reward of theſe ſufferings; I, far from being rewarded, was again, in this country, kept a priſoner, and delivered over to thoſe by whom I had been plundered, as a man inſane!

Before my intended departure to ſeek my fortune, I fell ill, and ſickneſs almoſt brought me to the grave. The Empreſs, hearing of my condition, in her great clemency, ſent one of her own phyſicians and a charitable friar to my aſſiſtance; both of

whom

whom I was at laſt obliged to pay. My own doctor would have re-ſtored me much cheaper. This was to be favoured, diſtinguiſhed!

At this time I received, unſoli-cited, a major's commiſſion, for which I was obliged to pay the fees. Being excluded from actual ſervice, the title to me was of little value: my rank in the army had been at leaſt equal ten years before in other ſervice. The following words, in-ſerted in my commiſſion, are not un-worthy remark :—" Her Majeſty, in " conſequence of my fidelity and " zeal for her ſervice, ſo conſpicu-" ouſly demonſtrated during a long " impriſonment, my extraordinary " endowments, and exemplary vir-" tues, had been graciouſly pleaſed to " grant me, in the Imperial ſer-" vice, the rank of major."——The rank of major! —— From this pre-amble,

amble, who would not have expected either the rank of general, or the restoration of my great Sclavonian estates. I had been fifteen years a captain of cavalry, and now was I most graciously made an invalid major!——I was made an invalid major three and twenty years ago, and an invalid major I still remain! Let all that has been related be called to mind, the shameful manner in which I had been pillaged, and so repeatedly betrayed; let Vienna, Dantzic, and Magdeburg be remembered; and, at the same time, be this my promotion remembered also! Let it be farther known that the commission of major might be bought, by any boy, for a few thousand florins! Thirty thousand florins only, of the money I had been robbed of, would have purchased a colonel's commission; I should then

have

have been a companion for generals; enabled by my pay, I then might have educated children for the good of the state, and my promotion would have placed me beyond the persecutions and peculations of my enemies.

It was the interest of these I should be useless; and, therefore, I was made an invalid. During the thirty-six years that I have been in the service of Austria, I never had any man of rank, any great general, any minister, any president, my enemy, except Count Graffalkowitz, and he was only my enemy because he had conceived a friendship for my estates.

My private character was never calumniated, nor did any truly worthy man ever speak of me but with respect and compassion. Who were, who are, my enemies? —— Jesuits, monks,

monks, unprincipled advocates, wish-
ing to become my curators; referendaries, who died despicable, or now
live in houses of correction; or accountants, who purchased protectors,
to avoid dying by the hands of the
hangman. Such as live, live in dread
of a similar end; for the Emperor
Joseph is just, and able to discover
the truth. Alas! the truth is discovered too late; age has now really
rendered me an invalid. Men with
hearts so base, so vile, ought, indeed,
to become the scavengers of society,
that, terrified by their example, succeeding judges may not rack the
heart of the honest man, seize on the
possessions of the orphan and the
widow, and wholly expel virtue out
of Austria.

God for ever preserve all good
men, after me, from such judges!
Men of this character never fail to

have

have friends at court, worthy. of themselves. Some maid of honour's chamber-maid, some fire-lighter, some menial person, with minds well befitting their station, who shall have the cunning, at proper opportunities, to say, as they did of me, — "Trenck is a diſſatisfied, reſtleſs man; "complains of every thing; speaks "evil of princes; is ſtill more than "half a Pruſſian in his heart; denies "that the Auſtrian Ulans are capable "of killing and eating the whole Pruſ- "ſian army!" My ſpirits are wearied; my heart ſinks at the remembrance.

I recovered, ſought an audience, but this was no more to be obtained. I attended the levee of Prince Kaunitz. Not perſonally known to him, he, on his pinnacle of power, viewed in me a crawling inſect among the ſwarm beneath. I thought somewhat more proudly; thought myſelf

a man :

a man : my actions were upright,
and so should my body be. I quitted the apartment, and, at the door,
was congratulated, by the mercenary
Swifs-porter, on my good fortune,
of having obtained an audience !

I applied to the field-marshal,
from whom I received this remarkable answer :—" If you cannot pur-
" chafe, my dear Trenck, it will be
" impossible to admit you into actual
" service ; beside, you are too old
" to learn our very difficult ma-
" noeuvres." I was then thirty-seven.
I briefly replied, " Your excellence
" mistakes my character ; I did not
" come to Vienna, to serve as an
" invalid major. My curators have
" taken good care I should have no
" money to purchafe ; but, had I
" millions, I would never obtain
" rank in the army by that mode."
I quitted the room with a shrug.—

The

The next day I addressed a memorial to the Emprefs, which, had I room, might here deferve to be wholly inferted. I did not re-demand my Sclavonian eftates, I only petitioned,

First—That thofe who had carried off quintals of filver and gold, from the premifes, and had rendered no account, either to me or the treafury, fhould be obliged to refund at leaft a part.

Secondly—That they fhould be obliged to return the thirty-fix thoufand florins, which had been illegally fequeftered from my family inheritance, and applied to a hofpital.

Thirdly—That the thirty-fix thoufand florins might be repaid, which Count Graffalkowitz had deducted from the allodial eftates, for three thoufand fix hundred pandours, who had fallen in the fervice of the Emprefs: I not being in juftice bound to pay for the lives of men, out of my private purse, who had died gloriously in defence of the Empress.

Fourthly—I required that fifteen thousand florins which had been deducted from my capital, and applied to the Bohemian fortifications, should, likewise, be restored, together with the fifteen thousand which had been unduely paid to the regiment of Trenck.

Fifthly—I reclaimed the twelve thousand florins, which I had been robbed of at Dantzic, by the treachery of the Imperial resident, Abramson; and public satisfaction from the magistracy of Dantzic, who had delivered me up, so contrary to the laws of nations, to the Prussian power.

These articles, and others, contained in the memorial, were indisputable claims, not being included

in

in the renunciation I had, some weeks before, been obliged to sign.

I, likewise, claimed the customary interest of six per cent. for the capital of seventy-six thousand florins, detained by the Hungarian chamber, which would amount to twenty thousand florins; I having been allowed only five per cent. and at last four.

I more particularly insisted on the restoration of my Sclavonian estates, and a proper allowance for improvements, which the very sentence of the court had granted, and which amounted to eighty thousand florins.

I intreated! I petitioned an arbitrator; I humbly solicited justice concerning incontrovertible rights, but nothing I obtained, not so much as an answer to this and a hundred other similar petitions!

I must

I muſt here ſpeak of my accountants, and of tranſactions during my
impriſonment. — I had bought a
houſe in Vienna, in the year 1750,
ſituated in the Teinfaltſtraſſe; the
price was ſixteen thouſand florins,
thirteen thouſand of which I had
paid at different inſtalments. The
receipts were among my writings.:
theſe writings, together with my
other effects, were taken from me at
Dantzic, in the year 1754. The colonel and quarter-maſter and all perſons
of the regiment, of whom I might re-
quire any account, were dead, in the
interim, nor have I, to this hour,
been able to learn more than that
my writings were ſent to the adminiſtrators of my affairs at Vienna.
With reſpect to my horſes, effects, and
property at Dantzic, in what manner theſe were diſpoſed of no one
could or would ſay.

After

After being releafed from my dungeon at Magdeburg, I inquired concerning my houfe, but no longer
found it mine. Thofe who had got-
ten poffeffion of my writings muft
have reftored the acquittances to the
feller, confequently, he could re-
demand the whole fum. My houfe,
however, was in other hands, and I
was brought in debtor fix thoufand
florins, for intereft and cofts of fuit.
Thus were houfe and money for-
ever gone, beyond redemption !—
Whom can I accufe ?

Again.—I had two years maintained, at my own expence, Lieutenant Schroeder, who had deferted from Glatz, and for whom I
afterwards obtained a captain's commiffion in the guard of Prince Efter-
hazy, at Eifenftadt. His own mif-
conduct caufed him to be cafhiered
and become a beggar. In my ad-

miniftrators

miniſtrators accounts I found the following article :

" To Captain Schroeder, for capi-
" tal, intereſt, and coſts of ſuit, ſix-
" teen hundred florins."

It was certain, I was not a penny indebted to this perſon : I, however, had no redreſs, having been, as before related, obliged to paſs, and ſign, all their accounts. –

I, four years afterward, obtained information concerning this affair : I met Schroeder, by accident, as he was aſking alms, near St. Stephen's; knew him, took him home with me, and enquired whether he had actually received theſe ſixteen hundred florins. He anſwered in the affirmative. " No one believed
" you would ever more have ſeen the
" light. I knew you had a friendſhip
" for me, and would willingly ſerve
                              " me,

" me, and, all being loſt to you, that
" you would give ſomething to relieve
" my extreme neceſſities. I went and
" ſpoke to Dr. Berger; he agreed we
" ſhould halve the ſum, and his
" contrivance was, I ſhould make oath
" I had lent you a thouſand florins,
" without having received your note.
" The money was paid me by M.
" Frauenberger, to whom I muſt
" ſend a preſent of Tokay, for Ma-
" dam Huttner."

Oh! Excellent! This was the manner in which my curators took care of
my property! Many ſimilar inſtances
I could produce, but I am too much
agitated by the recollection. I muſt,
however, ſpeak a word concerning
who and what my curators were.

The court counſellor, Kempf, was
my adminiſtrator, and counſellor
Huttner my referendary. The ſub-

ftitute of Kempf was Frauenberger, who, being obliged to act as a commiffary clerk, at Prague, during the war, could not attend to affairs at Vienna, but appointed one Krebs as a fub-fubftitute: whether M. Krebs had alfo a fub-fub-fubftitute, is more than I am able to fay.

Doctor Bertracker was *Fidei commiffcurator*, though there was no legal *Fidei commiffum* exifting. Doctor Berger, as Fidei commiff-advocate, was fuperintendent over them all, and, to them all, falaries werè to be paid.

Let us now fee what was the weighty bufinefs this noble company had to tranfact. I had feventy-fix thoufand florins in the Hungarian chamber, the intereft of which was yearly to be received, and added to the capital: this was their whole employment, and this

was

was certainly so trifling that any honest man would have performed it gratis. Kempf, having, luckily, got a fat capon, wished to pluck it in company with his old croney; he, therefore, gave him an office. The war made money scarce, and the discounting of bills with my ducats was a profitable trade to my curators. Had it been properly and honestly employed, I should, certainly, have found my capital increased, after my ten years imprisonment, full sixty thousand florins. Instead of these, I received three thousand florins at Prague, and nothing more; and, in compensation, found my capital diminished seven thousand florins.

Frauenberger and Berger died rich; and, the superior being obliged to protect him whom he had employed as a deputy, I must be eter-

nally

nally confined as a madman, left this worthy deputy fhould have been proved a rogue. This is the clue to the acquittal I was obliged to fign. Madam K—— was, at that time, a lady of the bedchamber at court: fhe could approach the throne; her chamber employments, indeed, procured her the keys of doors that, to me, were eternally locked.

Not fatisfied with this, Kempf applied to the Emprefs, informed her they were, indeed, acquitted, but not recompenfed, and that Frauenberg required four thoufand florins for remuneration. The Emprefs laid an interdict on the half of my income and penfion. Thus was I obliged to live in poverty, thus banifhed the Auftrian dominions, where my feventy-fix thoufand florins were reduced to fixty-three, the intereft of which I could only

only receive, and that burthened by the above interdict, the *Fidei commiſſum*, and adminiſtratorſhip. Of all theſe exactions, none ſo nearly, ſo much, affected me, as that of being obliged to preſent four thouſand florins to the man by whom my affairs had been thus adminiſtered.

The Empreſs, indeed, during my ſickneſs, ordered, as an eſpecial favour, that my captain's pay, during my ten year's impriſonment, ſhould be given me, amounting to eight thouſand florins ; which pay ſhe alſo ſettled on me as a penſion. By this penſion, however, I never profited ; for, during twenty-three years, that and more was ſwallowed by journies to Vienna, chicanery of courtiers, agents, advocates, and coſts of ſuit. Of the eight thouſand florins three were ſtolen during my illneſs ; the

court

court phyfician muft be paid thrice as much as another, and what remained, after my recovery, was funk in the preparations I made, to feek my fortune elfewhere. I had, befide, eight thoufand florins to repay, which had been advanced by my friends while in my dungeon; four thoufand of which were fent to General Riedt at Berlin.

Thus have I been rendered fo poor that I have never been able to repay my fifter's children the money their mother advanced, while my kind friends, at Vienna, have dignified me with the name of a difcontented man.

How far my captain's pay was matter of right, or matter of favour, let the world judge, being told I went in the fervice of Vienna to the city of Dantzic. Neither did this reftitution of pay equal the fum I

had

had fent the imperial minifter to obtain my freedom. It has been afferted the Emprefs delivered me from imprifonment. But no, I pofitively declare the contrary. I remained nine months in my dungeon after the articles were figned, unthought of, and, when mentioned, by the Auftrians, the King had twice rejected the propofal of my being fet free. The affair actually happened as follows, according to the account I received from their royal highneffes Prince Henry, Prince Ferdinand of Brunfwick, and, particularly, from the minifter, Count Hertzberg. General Riedt had received my ten thoufand florins full fix months, and feemed to remember me and my imprifonment no more. One Gala day, however, on the 21ft of December, the King happened to be in an extraordinary

good

good humour, and her majefty the Queen, the Princefs Amelia, and the prefent monarch, faid to the imperial minifter——" This is a fit opportu-" nity for you to fpeak in behalf of " Trenck." He, accordingly, waited his time, did fpeak, and the King replied, " Yes."

The joy of the whole company appeared fo great that Frederic, *the Great*, was offended!

Other circumftances, which contributed to promote this affair, the reader will eafily collect from my hiftory. That there were perfons in Vienna who earneftly defired to detain me in prifon is indubitable, from their proceedings after my return. My friends at Berlin, my own exertions, and my money, were my deliverers.

For fome weeks after I firft obtained my freedom, I was generally
abfent

abſent in mind, and deep in thought. This was a habit I had acquired in priſon, and the objects of ſight appeared but as the viſions of ſleep. I often ſtopped in the ſtreets, ſtared around me, doubted my own exiſtence, and bit my finger, in order to convince myſelf I was really awake and alive.

How trifling, how inſignificant, does the poor pageantry of greatneſs appear to me at this time! A thouſand people, variouſly bedecked in all their finery, wait expecting the appearance of ſome extraordinary perſonage! The doors are thrown open! An elderly matron enters! Graciouſly ſmiles, and every body moſt humbly ſmiles alſo! She aſks a few queſtions, concerning the wind and weather, of an old prieſt in a red cap and ſtockings, then addreſſes herſelf to an inſignificant Eſop, on whom all

eagerly

eagerly prefs forward to fawn ! The good Lady retires, and the hubbub of the fynagogue enfues, and this is called a levee ! Nor to this fublime honour. may men of honeſt hearts, the friends of virtue, or their country, find admittance : they have not the proper key, or, having it, hold it in contempt. Oh, man ! What art thou when called great and honourable ! What art thy thoughts, what thy dreams ! Doſt thou call thyſelf a man of reaſon, a philoſopher? What doſt thou then at courts ?——— By me they have long been avoided.

Walking round the ramparts of Vienna, having recovered from my ficknefs, the vivifying fpring, and the broad expanfe of heaven, infpired a confcioufnefs of prefent freedom and of pleafure indefcribable. I heard the morning fong of the lark. My heart palpitated, my

pulfe

pulfe quickened, the blood trickled through my veins with delight, for I felt I was a man, and recollected I was not in chains. Happen, faid I, what may, I fear not futurity fo long as my feet, my will, and my heart, are free, and, like yonder lark, I can remove from land to land. My foul poured forth its thankfulnefs for this confcioufnefs of freedom, and I determined to fly Vienna, and feek fome corner of the world where virtue has nothing to fear from the tongues of flanderers, the commands of courts, or the arbitrary will of monarchs.

If I went into any large companies, their prattle fo diftracted my mind, and the lights fo overpowered my eyes, that I returned home with head-ach, laffitude, and melancholy.

An accident happened which furthered my project. Marfhal Laudohn was going to Aix la Chapelle,

M 6

to take the waters. I had always perfonally honoured and loved this general when he was no more than a captain of pandours in my coufin's regiment. He went to take his leave of the Countefs Paar; I was prefent; the Emprefs entered the chamber, and, the converfation turning on Laudohn's journey, faid to me, " The baths, alfo, are neceffary " to the re-eftablifhment of your " health, Trenck." I was ready, and followed him in two days, where we remained about three months.

Here we were ftared at as ftrange animals. All the world wifhed to fee him becaufe of his fame in war, and me becaufe of my fufferings. The fociety of this worthy general poured balm into my wounded foul. He was as well acquainted with Vienna as myfelf: his fortitude and

magna-

magnanimity had conquered his enemies. What he was he had made himfelf.

The mode of life at Aix la Chapelle and Spa pleafed me, where men of all nations meet, and where princes are obliged to mingle with perfons of all ranks, if they wifh to feek converfation, and would not renounce fociety. One day, here, procured me more pleafure, efteem, and friendfhip, than a whole life in Vienna.

I fcarcely had remained here a month before my ever good friend, the Countefs Paar, wrote to me that the Emprefs had provided for me, and would make my fortune as foon as I fhould return to Vienna. I endeavoured, by my agents, to difcover in what this good fortune confifted, but ineffectually. I hoped every thing from the Emprefs, who

well

well knew my hard deſtiny. The death of the Emperor Francis at Inſpruck occaſioned the return of General Laudohn, and I followed him, on foot, to Vienna.

By means of the Counteſs Paar, I obtained an audience in a few days. The Empreſs received me graciouſly, and ſaid to me, " I will prove to " you, Trenck, that I keep my word. " I have inſured your fortune ; I " will give you a rich and prudent " wife." I replied, " Moſt gracious " Sovereign, I cannot determine to " marry, and, if I could, my choice " is already made, at Aix la Cha- " pelle."——" How ! are you mar- " ried then ?"——" Not yet, pleaſe " your Majeſty."——" Are you pro- " miſed ?"——" Yes."——" Well, " well, no matter for that, I will " take care of that affair ; I am de- " termined on marrying you to the
" rich

" rich widow of M——, and she ap-
" proves my choice. She is a very
" good kind of woman, and has
" fifty thousand florins a year. You
" are in want of such a wife."

I was thunder-struck. This lovely bride was an old canting hypocrite, of sixty three, extremely covetous, and a termagant. I answered, " I " must frankly speak truth to your " Majesty; I cannot consent, did she " possess the treasures of the whole " earth. I seek happiness, and not " misery. I have made my choice, " and given my word of honour, " which, as an honest man, I must " not break." The angry Empress regarded me with contempt, and said, " Your unhappiness is your " own work. Act as you think " proper; I have done." Here my audience ended, and, thus dis- missed, I bade an eternal adieu to

any

any hope of reward from empreffes, and kings.

Had I been inclined to make my fortune, by marrying an old woman, I might, long before, in 1750, have married one in Holland, worth three millions. This propofal was to recompenfe me for the lofs of my Sclavonian eftates, and all my other innumerable afflictions. Compliance was, moreover, impoffible; I was beloved, in Aix la Chapelle, where mutual affection, reafon, beauty, worth, and an exalted mind, all promifed future happinefs.

I was not actually affianced, at that time, to my prefent wife, but love determined me to return, to improve an intimacy fo far advanced.

Marfhal Laudohn knew my miftrefs, and promoted the match. He was acquainted with my heart, and

the

the warmth of my paſſions, perceived I could not conquer the ſecret deſire of vengeance on men, by whom I had been ſo cruelly, ſo wickedly treated. He, and my friend, Profeſſor Gellert, whom I viſited at Leipſic, both adviſed me to take this mode of calming paſſions, that often inſpired projects too vaſt, and that, ſeeking tranquillity, I ſhould fly the commerce of the great.

This friendly counſel was ſeconded by my own wiſhes. I returned to Aix la Chapelle, in December, 1765, and married the youngeſt daughter of the former Burgomaſter De Broe. He was dead: he had lived on his own eſtate at Bruſſels, where my wife was born, and educated. He had been called to this honourable office, by the unanimous voice of the citizens of Aix la Chapelle. He was

the

the defcendant of an ancient and noble family, in the province of Artois; and fome of his predeceffors, who poffeffed eftates near Aix la Chapelle, had, I know not for what reafon, accepted the dignity of knights of the Roman Empire. My wife's mother was fifter to the vice-chancellor of Duffeldorf, Baron Roberte, Lord of Roland.

It is not generally known, at Vienna, that one of the two Burgo-mafters of Aix la Chapelle muft always be elected from a noble family, and the other from the citizens. My children, therefore, can prove their defcent to be noble, both by the male and female line.

My wife has been with me in moft parts of Europe, where fhe has always been efteemed as fhe deferved. She then was young, handfome, worthy and virtuous, has

borne

borne me eleven children, all of whom she has nursed herself; eight of them are still living, and have been properly educated. God grant I may be enabled ever to provide for her as she deserves, and as is my duty. Two and twenty years has she borne a part in all my sufferings, and well deserves reward.

During my late short abode at Vienna, I made one effort more, I sought an audience from the present Emperor Joseph, related all that had happened to me, and particularly remarked such defects as I had observed in the government and regulations of the country. He gave me an attentive hearing, proved his desire to increase the happiness of his people, and commanded me to commit my thoughts to writing. This I accordingly performed, stating, with precision, and unreserve,

the

the obfervations I had made on affairs, civil, military, and econo-
mical.

Might I publifh this writing, I
am perfuaded it would do me no
difhonour, but, on the contrary, fhew
the monarch has, long fince, profited, by many of the improvements
therein fuggefted. My memorial
was gracioufly received ; all I petitioned for was fecrecy, having
therein named feveral perfons, who
were again capable of making me
wretched. I, farther, gave a more
ample account of what had happened to me in various countries,
and which prudence has occafioned
me to exprefs more cautioufly, and
darkly, in thefe pages. My memorial, though gracioufly received,
produced no effect, and I haftened
back to Aix la Chapelle.

For fome few years, I lived here
in

in peace; my houfe was the rendezvous of the firft people, who came
to take the waters. I began to be
more known, and every where procured myfelf friends, among the
very firft, and beft people.

I alfo vifited Profeffor Gellert at
Leipfic, fhewed him my manufcripts,
and afked his advice, concerning
what branch of literature he thought
it was probable I might beft fucceed
in. He moft approved my fables
and tales, but blamed the exceffive
freedom, with which I fpoke, in my
political writings. I neglected his
advice, and many enfuing calamities
were the confequence.

My wife brought me a fon in
December 1766, and I took this
opportunity of writing to the youthful monarch at Vienna. Though
publifhed in my writings, under the
title of Belifarius to the Emperor
Juftinian,

Juftinian, I think it neceffary to infert what follows here.

" Your Majefty is informed of " my marriage. My wife has borne " me a fon, whom I have chriftened " Jofeph. The imperial chamber- " lain, Colonel and Baron Rippenda, " ftood fponfor, by proxy, for your " Majefty. This was done with- " out firft obtaining your Majefty's " confent. I flattered myfelf your " Majefty would gracioufly be pleaf- " ed, thus far, to honour me, know- " ing my loyalty, and my misfor- " tunes. It is, indeed, my hope " that my conduct will procure " from your Majefty a more happy " futurity. This fon I fhall educate " in the fame loyal principles, and, " rather than depart from them, he " fhall imbibe poifon from his mo- " ther's breaft. —

" Moft gracious Emperor, while

" I live

" I live he will be provided for, but,
" at my death, then muft he fay to
" his fovereign, I am the fon, and
" rightful heir, of both the Trencks,
" whofe lands, and poffeffions, have
" been feized, by ftrangers, and ali-
" ens. I look up to you, gracious
" Sovereign, as a protecting Deity
" for my poor children. May your
" Majefty participate my joy, and
" gracioufly welcome this new citi-
" zen of the world. May it alfo
" pleafe you to inform me whe-
" ther it be your gracious pleafure
" I fhould farther prefent my
" thoughts in writing, for your high
" infpection. My enemies at Vi-
" enna daily increafe in ftrength,
" but on your fovereign protection
" I rely, and, whatever may be my
" fate, fhall, moft faithfully, and
" eternally, remain the loyal fervant
" of

" of my Emperor and my coun-
" try.

"TRENCK."

I have, at prefent, my reafons for inferting the following anfwer, which was written by the Emperor's own hand, and is ftill in my poffeffion.

" *Dear Major Trenck*,

" I am well pleafed that you have
" chriftened your fon Jofeph, and
" have chofen Colonel Rippenda as
" my proxy. As a proof of my
" good wifhes toward you, I have,
" for manifeft reafons, ordered that,
" henceforth, you fhall receive your
" pay at Bruffels, inftead of Vienna.
" Continue to fend me your writ-
" ings; I am pleafed to be in-
" formed of the truth; but they
" will give me more fatisfaction,
" fhould you fend them fimple and
                              " unadorned,

" unadorned, than in their former
" fatirical drefs.

" I am yours,

" J O S E P H."

I foon afterward received orders
to correfpond with his Majefty's private fecretary, Baron Roder; what
this correfpondence was muft not
here be told: fuffice it to fay, my
attempts to ferve my country were
fruftrated; I faw defects too clearly,
fpoke my thoughts too frankly,
and wanted fufficient humility ever
to obtain favour.

In the year 1767 I wrote the
Macedonian Hero, which became as
famous throughout all Germany as
my *Eulenfpiegel.* (The Malicious
Wag.) The poem did me honour,
but entailed new perfecutions; yet,
having wrote it, I never could re-

pent: I have had the honour of pre-
fenting it to five reigning princes,
by none of whom it has been burnt.
The Emprefs, alone, was highly
enraged. I had fpoken as Nathan
did to David, and the Jefuits now
openly became my enemies.

The following vile trick was
played me in the year 1768. A
friend, in Bruffels, was commiffioned
to receive my quarterly pay, from
whom I learnt an interdict had been
laid upon it by the court called Hofkriegfrath, at Vienna, in which I
had been condemned to pay a note
of feven hundred florins to one
Buffy, with fourteen years intereft.

Buffy was a known fwindler. I
was confcious no man on earth had
any fuch claim: I, therefore, jour-
neyed, poft-hafte, to Vienna. No
hearing, no fatisfactory account was
to be obtained. The anfwer was:

Res

Res jam judicata est; sentence is past, therefore all further attempts are too late.

I applied to the Emperor Joseph, pledged my honour, and my head, to prove the falsification of this note; and intreated a revision of the cause. My request was granted, and my attorney, Weyhrauch, was an upright man. When he began to speak, and request a day of revision to be appointed, he was threatened to be committed by the referendary, Zetto, should he undertake to interfere and defend the affairs of Trenck. He answered, firmly, " His defence is " my business in this place: I know " my cause to be good." Silence was imposed, and nothing further done.

Four months did I continue in Vienna before the day was appointed

to

to revise this cause. It now appeared evidently there were erasures and
holes through the paper, in three
places: all in court were convinced
the claim ought to be annulled, and
the claimant punished. Zetto, not-
withstanding, ordered the parties to
withdraw, and then so managed that
the judges resolved the case must be
again laid before the court, with formal written proofs.

This gave time for new knavery:
I was obliged to return to Aix la
Chapelle, and four years elapsed before this affair, clear as the meridian
sun, was decided. Two priests, in
the interim, who were such as father confessors to convents usually
are, took false oaths that they had
actually seen me receive the money.
At length, however, I proved that
the note was dated a year after I had
been imprisoned at Magdeburg, I,

con-

confequently, could not give any fuch note in Vienna. Nay, farther, my attorney proved the very writs of the court had, likewife, been falfified. Zetto, the referendary, and Buffy, were abfolutely the forgers, but I happened to be too active, and my attorney too honeft, to lofe this caufe. I was obliged to make three very expenfive journies from Aix la Chapelle to Vienna, left judgment fhould go by default. Sentence at laft was neceffarily pronounced; I gained my caufe, and the note was declared a forgery, but the cofts, amounting to three thoufand five hundred florins, I was obliged to pay, for Buffy could not; nor was he corporally punifhed, though at laft driven from Vienna for his villainous acts. Zetto, however, ftill continued referendary, ftill continued, for eighteen years, my barbarous perfecutor; till, not long

 fince,

since, he was deprived of his office, and condemned to the house of correction.

May no such judgments ever again be given in courts at Vienna; where, perhaps, I am the only one whose perseverance and courage would have demonstrated their injustice. But this perseverance, this courage, have made these courts my enemies, as I have since bitterly experienced. Too late was Zetto punished for the welfare of many a widow and orphan, and still are numerous of his vile practices unknown.

This cause excited many remarks at Vienna; I gained much honour, but more expence and trouble. I took this opportunity to solicit justice in my other affairs, but to little purpose, except that the world be-

gan

gan to know me better, and afford me somewhat more of its pity.

My knowledge of the world increased at Aix la Chapelle, where men of all nations and characters met, particularly English. In the morning I might converse with a lord in opposition, in the afternoon with an orator of the King's party; and at night with an honest man of no party. In conversation like this knowledge is acquired and imparted. I sent Hungarian wine into England, France, Holland, and the Empire; this occasioned me to undertake long journies, and as my increase of acquaintance gave me opportunities of receiving many foreigners with politeness in my own house, I was, myself, also, well received whereever I went.

The income I should have had from Vienna was all ingulphed by

law-

law-suits, curators, attornies, and the journies I was obliged to undertake; having been thrice cited to appear, in person, before the Hofkriegsrath. To me nothing remained; I was described as a dangerous malecontent, who had deserted his native land, by which insinuations my enemies took care to profit. I, neverthelefs, remained, be the country in which I lived what it would, an honeft man; one who could provide for his own neceffities without meannefs or the favour of courts; one whofe acquaintance was every where efteemed. In Vienna, alone, was I unsought, unemployed, and obfcure.

My love of the chace made me particularly acceptable to the English, who brought with them their own horfes and dogs, to hunt the wolf and wild boar, animals not to be found in their own country. I,

in

in return, paffed whole fummers at their country feats in England, Scotland, and Ireland, and thus obtained a thorough knowledge of the nation.

The Elector Palatine had granted me a certain extent of country in the territory of Juliers, where I might hunt, and the Count Palatine of the Rhine gave me permiffion to hunt where I pleafed. To defend this right of hunting was now my duty, and occafioned various difputes; thefe, however, were not often determined in courts of law, but, ufually, every man afferted his claim with his fword.

One day an accident happened, on this occafion, which made me renowned over the country as a magician, as one whom lead could not penetrate, and who had power over fogs and clouds.

N 5

I had

I had a quarrel with the Palatine prefident, Baron Blankart, concerning a hunting diftrict, I, therefore, wrote to him that, on a certain day, he fhould repair to the fpot in difpute, whither I would alfo come, at ten in the morning, with fword and piftol, hoping he would there give me fatisfaction for the affront I had received. Hither I went, with two huntfmen, and two friends, but, inftead of the baron, was aftonifhed to find two hundred armed peafants affembled.

What was to be done? I fent one of my huntfmen to the army of the enemy, informing them that, did they not beat a retreat, I fhould fire. It was in the month of Auguft, the day was clear and fine, and, fuddenly, a thick and impenetrable fog arofe. My huntfman returned, with intelligence that, having delivered his

meffage

meſſage juſt as the fog came on, theſe valiant heroes had all run away in the greateſt fright.

I advanced, found nobody, fired my piece, as did my friends and followers, and marched to the manſion of my adverſary, where my hunting horn was blown in triumph, in his court-yard. The runaway peaſants fired at a diſtance, but the fog prevented their taking any aim.

Having taken this ſatisfaction, I returned home, where many falſe reports had preceded me. My wife expected I ſhould be brought home dead, and that many others would be maimed, however, not the leaſt miſchief had happened.

It ſoon was propagated through the country that I was a magician, had raiſed a fog to render myſelf invulnerable, and that the truth of

N 6   this

this could be juftified by two hundred eye witneffes. All the monks
of Aix la Chapelle, Juliers, and Co-
logn, publicly preached concerning
me, reviled me, and warned the people to beware of the arch-magician,
and lutheran, Trenck.

On a future occafion, this belief
I turned to matter of merriment. I
went to hunt the wolf in the exten-
five forefts of the county of Monjoye,
and invited the peafants and townf-
men to the chace. The firft day
we had but little fport; toward
evening I, and fome forty of my
followers, retired to reft in the neigh-
bouring charcoal huts, well provided
with wine and brandy. " My lads,"
faid I, " it is now neceffary you
" fhould all difcharge your pieces,
" and load them anew, that to-mor-
" row no wolf may efcape, and that
" none of you may excufe yourfelves

2   " on

" on your pieces miffing fire." The
guns were accordingly reloaded, and
placed in a feparate chamber, after
which, they began to eat, drink, and
dance. While they were merry-
making, my huntfman privately
went into this chamber, drew the
balls, and charged the pieces with
powder, various of which he loaded
with double charges. Some of their
notched balls I put into my pocket.

In the morning, away went I, and
my merry fellows, to the chace. As
we walked, their converfation turned
on my necromancy, and the miraculous manner in which I could
envelop myfelf in a cloud, or make
myfelf bullet proof. " What is
" that you are talking about, my
" lads ?" faid I. " Some of thefe
" unbelieving good folks," anfwered
my huntfman, " affirm your Ho-
" nour is unable to ward off balls."
" Well

" Well then," faid I, laughing, to one of them, " fire away, my good " fellow, and try." The man refuf-ed, and my huntfman took his piece out of his hand, and fired. I pretended to parry with my hand, and called, " Let any man, that is fo " inclined, fire, but only one at a " time." Accordingly, they began, and, pretending to twift and turn about, I fuffered them all to difcharge their pieces. It muft be remarked I was perfectly fecure, as my people had carefully noticed that no man had reloaded his gun. Some of them received fuch blows from the guns that were doubly charged, that they fell down, terrified in amazement, at the powers of magic. I advanced, holding in my hand fome of the marked balls. " Let " every one choofe his own," called I. All ftood motionlefs, and many of

them

them flunk home, with their guns on their fhoulders; fome few remained, and our fport was excellent.

On Sunday the monks of Aix la Chapelle again began to preach. My black art became the theme of the whole country, and, at this day, many of the people prefent will make oath that they fired upon me, and that, after catching them in my hand, I returned the balls.

Thus eafy is it to gull this wife world. My high and invulnerable qualities were publifhed throughout Juliers, Aix la Chapelle, Maeftricht, and Cologne, and perhaps this belief has more than ten times faved my life; the priefts having propagated it, from their pulpits, in a country which fo fwarms with highway robbers that one hundred and fixty men have been broken alive on the wheel, quartered, and burnt,

within

within a year, and where, for a single ducat, any man may hire an affaſſin.

It is indeed no ſmall matter of ſurpriſe that I ſhould, for years, have preſerved my life in a town, where there are twenty-three monaſteries and churches, and where the monks are all adored as ſo many deities. The catholic clergy had been ſufficiently enraged againſt me, by my poem of " The Macedonian Hero ;" and, in 1772, I publiſhed a newſpaper at Aix la Chapelle, and another periodical work entitled, " The " Friend of Men," in which I endeavoured to unmaſk hypocriſy. Indeed for me, an apoſtolic major of the apoſtolic Maria-Thereſa, to write thus in a town ſwarming with friars, and in a tone ſo undaunted, was unexampled.

At preſent, now toleration and
free-

freedom of opinion are more encouraged, by the Emperor, Joseph II. many such effayifts encounter bigotry and deceit with ridicule; or, wanting invention themfelves, publifh extracts from writings that belong to the age of Luther. I have the honour of having attacked the very pillars of the Romifh hierarchy in days more dangerous; I may boaft of being the firft German who, unprotected, raifed a fermentation on the Upper Rhine, and in the ftate of Auftria, fo advantageous to truth, the progrefs of the human underftanding, and the happinefs of futurity.

Let the world read and judge of my writings! They contain nothing inimical to the pure morality taught by Chrift. I attacked the fale of indulgences, the avarice of Rome, the lazinefs, deceit, licentious gluttony,

tony, robbery, and blood-fucking of
the monks of Aix la Chapelle, who
fought the murder of each other in
the very church, and in prefence of
the altar. I wrote as a moralift,
and morals do not enrich monks.
Therefore did the arch-prieft, and
nine of his coadjutors, declare, every
Sunday, from the pulpit, publickly
naming me, I was a free-thinker,
a wizard, one whom every man,
wifhing well to God and the Church,
ought to affaffinate. The Jefuit
Father Zünder declared I was invulnerable, and a day was appointed,
on which my writings were to be
burnt before my houfe, the houfe
itfelf erafed, and its inhabitants maf-
facred. My wife received letters,
warning her to fly with her children
for fafety, which warning fhe in
terror obeyed. I and two of my
huntfmen remained, provided with

eighty-

eighty-four loaded mulkets. Thefe I difplayed in the gallery before the window, that all might be convinced I would make a defperate defence. I lived oppofite the court houfe. The appointed day came, and Father Zünder, with my writings in his hand, attended by all the ftudents in the town, appeared ready for the attack; the other monks had incited the towns-people to a general ftorm; no man, however, had the heart to appear in the market place, while I ftood in a gallery fo well ftored with fire arms. Thus paffed the day and night in fufpenfe.

In the morning a fire broke out in the town. I haftened, fearlefs, with my two huntfmen, fecretly well armed, to give affiftance: we dafhed the water from our buckets, and all obeyed my directions. Father Zünder and his ftudents were there, likewife; I

approached

approached him by degrees, and ftruck his anointed ear with my leathern bucket, as if by accident, which no man thought proper to notice. I paffed undaunted through the crowd, the people all fmiled, pulled off their hats, and wifhed me a good morning. Such are the populace, when they perceive they are not feared. The people of Aix la Chapelle were ftupid bigots, but too cowardly to murder a man who was prepared for his own defence. Here the threats of my adverfaries for this time ended.

As I was riding to Maeftricht through a hollow-way, a ball whiftled by my ears, which, no doubt, was a meffenger fent after me by thefe perfecuting priefts.

When hunting near the convent of Schwartzenbruck, three Dominicans lay in ambufh for me behind a hedge.

a hedge. One of their colleagues, who often hunted with me, pointed out the place. I was on my guard with my double-barrelled gun, drew near, but called with a voice of terror—
" Shoot, fcoundrels! But do not
" kill me, for the devil ftands ready
" for you at your elbow!"—One fired, and they all ran ; the ball hit my hat. I fired, likewife, and wounded one defperately, whom the other two carried off: he recovered, however, and, afterward, eloped with a cow-girl.

Their attempts at poifoning me were all unfuccefsful, for I always ate at home. In the year 1774, journeying from Spa to Limbourg, I was attacked by eight banditti. The weather was rainy, and my mufket was in its cafe; my fabre was entangled in the belt, fo that, unable to draw it, I was obliged to defend myfelf as with a club. I fprang
from

from the carriage, and, with every effort of nature, fought in defence of my life, ftriking down all before me, while my faithful huntfman protected me behind. I difperfed my affailants, haftened to my carriage, and drove away. One of thefe fellows was, foon after, hanged, and owned, before execution, that the confeffor of this banditti had promifed perpetual abfolution, could they but difpatch me, but that no man could fhoot me, becaufe that Lucifer had rendered me invulnerable. Perfuaded of the truth of this, fortunately for me, they had only affaulted me with clubs. My ftrength and agility, fighting too for life, was fuperior to theirs, and they buried two of their gang, whom, with my heavy fabre, I had killed. I efcaped with a bruifed arm and fhoulder;

my

my huntfman received a violent blow with a ftone.

To fuch excefs of cruelty may the violence and rage of priefts be carried! Yet did not my writings contain a fingle word inimical to the pure morality of Chrift: I attacked only grofs abufes, the deceit and lafcivioufnefs of the monks of Aix la Chapelle, Cologne, and Liege, where they are worfe than canibals, wallowing, like fwine, in the flough of ignorance and gluttony. I wifhed to inculcate the true Chriftian duties among my fellow citizens, and the attempt was fufficient to irritate the felfifh church of Rome.

From my Emprefs I had nothing further to hope. Her confeffor had painted me, with all the craft of a prieft, as an arch-heretic, and a perfecutor of the holy and bleffed mother church. Nor was this all:
opi-

opinions were artfully propagated, through views that I was a restless man, dangerous to the community. Such, indeed, is the universal supposition of all who have neither personally known me, nor read my writings.

Hence, too, was I always wronged in courts of judicature, where there are ever found wicked or bigoted men. The latter thought they were serving the cause of God by injuring me; and the former are ever the enemies of pure and simple truth, undauntedly displayed, it being their interest that virtue and patriotism should fall the victims of falsehood. Yet were they unable to prevent my writings producing me much money, or being circulated through all Germany. The Aix la Chapelle Journal or Gazette became so famous, in the first year, that, in the second, I had

four

four thoufand fubfcribers, by each of whom I gained a ducat.

The poftmafters, who gain confiderably by circulating newfpapers, were envious, becaufe the Aix la Chapelle Gazette deftroyed feveral of the others, and, therefore, formed a combination.

I will briefly notice what fo much contributed to the fale of my paper. I was acquainted with moft countries and courts, in which I had the beft of correfpondents: wherefore, inftead of merely relating paft events, I could foretel future. I was, fometimes, obliged to be ambiguous, yet my meaning was very capable of being underftood.

Prince Charles of Sweden, eldeft brother of the prefent King, placed the greateft confidence in me during his refidence at Aix la Chapelle and Spa, and I accompanied him into

Holland. When I took my leave of him at Maeſtricht, while we were in the ſubterranean gallery of the fortifications, he ſaid to me, " When my father dies, either my " brother ſhall be king, or we will " loſe our heads." * The King died, and Prince Charles, ſoon after, ſaid, in the poſtſcript of one of his letters, " What we ſpoke of at Maeſ- " tricht will ſoon be fully accom- " pliſhed, and you may then come " to Stockholm."

On this I inſerted an article in my Gazette, declaring a revolution had taken place in Sweden, and that the king had made himſelf abſolute. The other papers thought proper to expreſs their doubts, and I, im-

* The prince meant to ſay the power of his father was ſo limited that he was not a king. The preſent monarch has taken care to have no ſuch complaint. T.

medi-

mediately, offered to wager a thoufand ducats on the truth of every
article publifhed in my Gazette under the title " Aix la Chapelle." The
news of the revolution in Sweden
was inftantaneoufly confirmed. This
incident added greatly to the authen-
ticity of my paper.

My Gazette foretold the Polifh
partition fix weeks fooner than any
other; but how I obtained this intelligence muft not here be mentioned. I, alfo, was active in the
defence of Queen Matilda of Den-
mark.

The French miniftry were highly
offended at the following pafqui-
nade: " The three eagles have rent
" the Polifh bear; without lofing a
" feather, with which any man in
" the cabinet of Verfailles can write.
" Since the death of Mazarine, they
" write there only with goofe quills."

By

By defire of the King of Poland, I wrote a narrative of the attempt made to affaffinate him, and named the nuncio, who had given a general abfolution to the confpirators in the chapel of the holy virgin.

The houfe was now in flames. Rome infifted I fhould recal my words. Her nuncio, at Cologne, vented poifon, daggers, and excommunication : the Emprefs-Queen, herfelf, thought proper to interfere. I obtained from Warfaw a copy of the examination of the confpirators for my juftification. This I threatened to publifh, and ftood, unmoved, in the defence of truth. I derived new honour, but new perfecutors, likewife; as for protectors none : mine was the fate of all reformers, who muft expect reward beyond the grave.

The Emprefs wrote to the poft-mafter general of the empire, commanded

manded him to lay an interdict on the Aix la Chapelle Gazette. Informed of this, I ended its publication with the year, but wrote an essay on the partition of Poland; which, also, did but increase my enemies. The priests took care not to be idle at these moments.

The magistracy of Aix la Chapelle is elected from the lower ranks of people, and the Burger's court consists of an ignorant rabble. I know no exceptions, but Baron Lamberte and De Witte; and, to heighten the ridicule, this people assume to themselves titles of dignity, for which they are amenable to the fiscal court at Vienna. Knowing I found little protection at Vienna, they imagined they might attack and drive me from their town. I was a spy on their evil deeds, of whom they would willingly have rid themselves.

I, like-

I, likewife, knew that the two fheriffs, Klofs and Furth, and the recorder, Geyer, had robbed the town-chamber of forty-thoufand dollars, and divided the fpoil. To thefe I was a dangerous man; for fuch reafons, they fought a quarrel with me, pretending I had committed a trefpafs by breaking down a hedge, and fent a fergeant, citing me to appear at their town-houfe.

It is a well-known right of the empire, that no magiftrate of thefe courts can enforce the perfonal appearance of a ftaff-officer. I was fubject only to the court called Hofkriegfrath, at Vienna. But by this court they foon underftood I fhould not be protected. A moft difagreeable litigation enfued. By accident I obtained a letter from Count Gravenitz, member of the Aulic council, to the poftmafter, Heinfberg,

berg, with whom I had alſo a ſuit pending, in which he ſaid that, though juſtice was on my ſide, he would undertake to weary me by procraſtination: he fulfilled his promiſe, and my wife was obliged to pay three hundred florins of gold, under pain of execution, while I was abſent at Vienna, endeavouring to obtain right.

This was a trifle. The poſtmaſter, Heinſberg, of Aix la Chapelle, although he had two thouſand three hundred rix-dollars of mine in his poſſeſſion, inſtituted falſe ſuits againſt me, on pretence of a note, which was nothing more than a receipt, for a thouſand dollars on account, obtained verdicts againſt me contrary to the moſt clear and evident juſtice, ſeized on a cargo of wine, worth three thouſand eight hundred dollars, at Cologne, and I, on the whole,

in-

incurred loffes to the amount of eighteen thoufand florins, exclufive of the interruption given to the trade I carried on in wine; which devoured the fortune of my wife, and by which fhe, with myfelf, and my children, were reduced to poverty.

Let it not be imagined thefe are merely affertions. The prefident of one of the courts, to whom I complained, after moralizing concerning the vanity of earthly, and the reality of heavenly, hopes, in a letter told me, " It might be the will of God " that I fhould be treated with in- " juftice. He could afford me no " help, for he had received her " majefty's commands."————The referendary, Gravenitz, himfelf, in 1778, with tears in his eyes, acknowledged how much he had injured me, affirmed he had been deceived, and promifed he would

2   endea-

endeavour to obtain reftitution. I
was moved, and forgave him, and
he attempted to keep his promife;
but his power declined, his corrupt-
nefs had been manifeft, the bribes
he had received were become too
public. He was, at length, difpoffeffed of his poft, but, alas! too
late for me. He now lives, like the
greater part of my enemies, a banifhed man in Poland, defpifed, and
in poverty. Two other of my judges
are at this time obliged, in chains, to
fweep the ftreets of Vienna, where
they are condemned to the houfe of
correction. Had this been their employment, inftead of being feated on
the feat of judgment, twenty years
ago, I might have been more fortunate. It certainly is a remarkable
circumftance that I fhould fo often
and fo continually have been de-
fpoiled by unjuft judges. Who

O 5   would

would have dared to have publifhed their deferts during the plenitude of their power? Who would have had the temerity to affirm their evil fhould hereafter bring them to attend on the city fcavenger? I, indeed, knew them but too well, and, fearlefs, fpoke what I knew. But I was a reftlefs man! A flanderer of imperial courts of juftice I! It was my misfortune, not my fault, that I was acquainted with their mal-practices fooner than my gracious fovereign.

Here let the fcene clofe on my litigations at Aix la Chapelle and Vienna. May God preferve every honeft man from the like! True it is they hang heavy on my heart. They have fwallowed up my own property, and that of my innocent wife. Enough! Enough!

From the year 1774 to 1777 I chiefly fpent my time in journeying

through

through England and France.   I
was intimate with Dr. Franklin, the
American minifter; alfo, with the
Counts St. Germain and Vergennes,
who made me advantageous propo-
fals to go to America; but I was
prevented accepting them by my
affection for my wife and children.

. My kind friend, the Landgrave of
Heffe-Caffel, who had been governor
of Magdeburg during my imprifonment, offered me a commiffion in
his fervice among the troops going
to America : but I anfwered—

"Gracious prince, my heart beats
"in the caufe of freedom only, I
"will never affift in enflaving men.
"Were I at the head of your brave
"grenadiers, I fhould revolt to the
"Americans."

During the year 1775 I continued,
at Aix la Chapelle, my periodical
effays, entitled, "The Friend of
O 6   "Men."

" Men." My writings had made some impreſſion; the people began to read; the monks were ridiculed, and became more humble : my partizans increaſed, and their arch-leader had the good fortune to get himſelf cudgelled.

They did not now mention my name publicly, but catechiſed their penitents at confeſſion. During this year various ſimple people came to me from Cologne, Bonn, and Duſſeldorf, deſiring to ſpeak with me in private. When I inquired their buſineſs, they told me their clergy had informed them I was propagating a new religion, in which every man muſt ſign himſelf over to the devil, who, then, would ſupply them with money. They were willing to become converts to my faith, would Beelzebub but give them money, and revenge them on their prieſts. " My

" good

" good friends," anſwered, I, " your " teachers have deceived you: I "know of no devils but themſelves. " Were it, indeed, true that I was " founding a new religion, the con- " verts to which the devil would ſup- " ply with money, your biſhops and " prieſts would be the very firſt of " my apoſtles, and the moſt catholic. " I am an honeſt moral man, my wor- " thy friends, as a Chriſtian ought to " be. Go home, in God's name, and " do your duty. Be honeſt and in- " duſtrious, and you will not then " want the devil to bring you money."

I forgot to mention in its place that the recorder or preſident of the ſheriff's court at Aix la Chapelle, who is the ſon of the banker Geyer, and who is called Baron Geyer, had aſſociated himſelf, in 1778, with a Jew convert, and a knight of induſ- try; and that this noble company,

in

in concert, swindled a Dutch merchant out of eighty thousand florins,
by assuming the arms of the Elector,
Palatine, and producing forged receipts and contracts. Geyer was
taken in Amsterdam, and would
have been hanged, but that, by the
aid of a faithful servant, he effected
his escape. He returned to Aix la
Chapelle, where he enjoys his honourable office.—Three years ago it
was proved he had robbed the town-
chamber. His handsome wife was,
at that time, *generis communis,* and
procured him powerful friends at
court. The assertions of this worthy
gentleman found greater credit at
Vienna than those of the innocent,
the injured Trenck. Oh, Shame!
Shame!——Oh, World! World!
World!

My wine trade was so successful
that I had correspondents and stores

in

in London, Paris, Bruxelles, Hamburg, and the Hague, and had gained forty-thoufand florins, with the moft flattering profpects from England. One unfortunate day deftroyed all my fuccefsful hopes in this traffic.

Being in London, I was defrauded of eighteen hundred guineas by a fwindler. The relating of this ftory will do but little honour to the Englifh nation. The fault was, principally, my brother-in-law's, a young man, who parted with the wine before he had received the money. In England there is no law againft fuch deceivers. They bid you truft no-body, you will then not be wronged. And when I had been wronged, and afked my friend's affiftance, I was only laughed at; as if they were happy that an Englifhman had the wit to cheat a German.

I can-

I cannot give a circumftantial hiftory of this affair, but it is neceffary to narrate it in the abftract, our prejudices being fo ftrong in favour of the great worth and juftice of the Britifh nation.

Finding myfelf defrauded of my wine, I haftened to Sir John Fielding. He was acquainted with me, told me he knew I had been fwindled, and that his friendfhip would make him active in my behalf; that he, alfo, knew the houfes where my wine was depofited, and that a party of his runners fhould go with me, fufficiently ftrong for its recovery. I was little aware that he had, at that time, two hundred bottles of my beft Tokay in his cellar. His pretended kindnefs was a fnare; he was in partnerfhip with robbers, the ftupid among whom only he hung, and preferved the

moft

moſt adroit for the promotion of trade.

He ſent a conſtable and ſix of his runners with me, commanding them to act under my orders. By good fortune I had a violent head-ach, and could not attend them myſelf, but ſent my brother-in-law, who ſpoke better Engliſh than I. Him they brought to the houſe of a Jew, and told him, " Your wine, ſir, is " here concealed." Though it was broad day, the door was locked, that he might be induced to act illegally. The conſtable deſired him to break the door open, which he, according-ly, did: the Jews, in a pretended fright, came running, and aſked— " What do you want, gentlemen ?" —" I want my wine," anſwered my brother. — " Take what is your " own," replied a Jew, " but be-

" ware

" ware of touching my property.

" I have bought the wine."

My brother attended the conſtable and runners into a cellar, and there found a great part of my wine. He wrote to Sir John Fielding, that he had found the wine, and deſired to know how he was to act. Fielding, by a verbal meſſage, anſwered—" It " muſt be taken by the owner."— My brother, accordingly, got a cart, and ſent me the wine.

He attended the runners, in like manner, to the houſe of another Jew, where they proceeded as before, and he came back quite rejoiced at having recovered the wine.

Next day came a conſtable, with a warrant, ſaying, " He wanted to " ſpeak with my brother, and that " it was to go to my friend, Sir " John Fielding." When he was in the ſtreet he touched him with

his

his ftaff, and told him—" Sir, you
" are my prifoner."—Here it muft
be remarked that no man can be
arrefted in his own houfe in London;
but that, when he is in the ftreet,
and the conftable has touched him
with his ftaff, he is beyond delivery;
and, fhould he run, would be ftopped
by the people.

All this I was a fpectator of through
the window, unable to give any affiftance. I went, however, to Sir
John Fielding, and afked what it all
meant. This upright juftice anfwered, in a magifterial tone—That
my brother had been accufed of fe-
lony. The Jews and fwindlers had
fworn the winë was a legal purchafe.
If I had not taken care to be paid,
or was ignorant of the Englifh laws,
that was my fault. Six fwindlers
had fworn the wine was paid for;
which circumftance he had not
known,

known, or he fhould not have granted me a warrant. My brother had,
alfo, broken open doors, and forcibly
taken away wine which was not his
own. They had legally made oath
of this, and he was charged with
burglary and robbery.

He farther defired me, immediately, to give bail in a thoufand
guineas for my brother, for his
appearance in the court of king's
bench; otherwife, his trial would
immediately come on, and in a few
days he would be hanged.

What was my rage at finding myfelf thus treated! And how willingly would I have plunged my fword
in the breaft of a man fo vile as this
chief magiftrate of London!

I haftened to a lawyer, who was
my friend, who confirmed what had
been told me, advifed me immediately to give bail, and he would then

defend

defend my caufe. I applied to Lord Mansfield, and received the fame anfwer. I told my ftory to all my great friends, who were, chiefly, members of parliament, and they laughed at me, that I fhould trade in London, without better underftanding the laws. My intimate friend, Lord Grofvenor, faid, " Send " more wine to London, and we " will pay you fo well that you will " foon recover your lofs."——This is the character of the nation. I am certain he would have kept his word, but I wanted the neceffary capital.

I went to my wine merchants, who had ftock in hand of mine worth upward of a thoufand guineas. They gave bail for my brother, and in four days he was releafed.

Fielding, in the interim, fent his runners

runners to my houfe, took back the wine, and reftored it to the Jews, as property of which they had been robbed. They threatened farther to profecute me as a receiver of ftolen goods. I fled, in all hafte, from London, through Dover, to Paris, where I immediately fold off my remaining ftock at half price, honoured my bills, and fo ended my merchandize.

My brother returned to London, in November, to defend his caufe in the court of king's bench; but the fwindlers had difappeared, and the lawyer required a hundred pounds to proceed. The conclufion of all this was, my brother returned, with feventy pounds lefs in his pocket, fpent as travelling expences; and the ftock, in the hands of my wine merchants, was detained on pretence of paying the bail. They brought me in an

apothe-

apothecary's bill, and all was loft. Thus do the Englifh treat the Germans, notwithftanding I had fo many friends in London.

I might fill a volume with fimilar inftances. I fhall only relate one fhort ftory. A German violin-maker, in London, intending to return home, had bought his wife a filver coffee-pot, which was left ftanding on the table in his chamber. Some one knocked at the door, and two Jews entered. One befpoke a violin, the other, while he was converfing, fnatched up the coffee-pot, and ran. The German looked round, and miffed the coffee-pot, but the other Jew told him, " Do not be uneafy, my friend, go " with me, and I will make my " comrade give you back your cof- " fee-pot. It is only fome trick : " he is a mad-headed fellow."

The

The poor German went with the Jew, who brought him into a chamber, where were four other Jews, and his coffee-pot on the table. He took it, and faid, " God be praifed, " I have found it once more." The Jew anfwered not a word; and the German returned home with his coffee-pot.—Forthwith went five Ifraelites to the juftice, and fwore that the German had entered their chamber, and ftolen thereout a filver coffee-pot. A conftable attended them to the German's houfe. The Jew faid, " That is my coffee-pot:" and the other fwearers anfwered, " Yes, " that is yours." The German was taken into cuftody, and, being deftitute of witneffes, was hung upon the evidence of the five Jews.

I fpoke with this poor fellow in prifon, who told me the ftory himfelf, and actually faw this honeft

man

man hung, by the pitylefs Englifh. What will my readers now fay to this high-efteemed nation, which, in reality, for a thoufand reafons, merits our contempt?

Enough of the proud and felfifh Britons, who would treat us, and all other nations, as they do their negroes, were we to fall under their dominion. *

Many

* The names of the wine merchants are omitted in the tranflation: the Baron may have been miftaken; they *may* have acted honeftly. There is no doubt of the Baron's veracity; that is, fpeaking from the conviction of his own mind. He was in England, and, as he himfelf afferts, moft fhamefully fwindled: thofe concerned have fince become notorious. The perplexities of law daily expofe the natives themfelves to the arts of the difhoneft. This is an inevitable defect, the confequence of an advantage, the value of which foreigners feldom underftand: they are, from temperament, more hafty than the Englifh; they have been accuf-

Many other particulars remain to be told of Aix la Chapelle, for which I have not sufficient room in this place.

The Swedish General Sprengporten came to Aix la Chapelle, in the year 1776.

tomed, in states less free, when injustice is manifest, to more summary proceedings; and, when they have any dispute in England, they usually fall into the very worst hands. Let us hope the Baron was misinformed, hasty, and that the memory of Sir John Fielding has been wronged! If not—!

The Baron so little knew how he was to act, that it is impossible, from his narrative, to say whether his brother was arrested as a debtor or imprisoned as a felon. His perplexity and distress inspire abhorrence for those instruments by whom, instead of vigorously protecting an uninformed stranger, they were increased. The liberal-minded Englishman will pardon his severity on the nation, remembering how he was treated; though by individuals whom this and every nation must pity and despise.

The

1776. He had planned and carried into execution the revolution fo highly favourable to the King, but had fuddenly left Sweden in difcontent, and came to take the waters with a rooted hypochondria.

He was the moft dangerous man in Sweden, and had told the King himfelf, after the revolution, in the prefence of his guards, " While " Sprengporten can hold a fword, " the King has nothing to com- " mand."

It was feared he would go to Ruffia, and Prince Charles wrote to

The ftory of the poor German and his coffee-pot, if the Baron was not deceived, is indeed a tragical one: yet would the oaths of five Jews have hung five hundred, or five thoufand, Englifhmen ; were they equally deftitute of the means to prove the falfity of fuch accufations. Not the laws, not the nation, wicked men only were guilty of this murder.   T.

me,

me, in the name of the monarch, defiring I would exert myfelf, to the utmoft, to make myfelf intimate with him, and perfuade him to return to Sweden. No tafk could have been more difficult. He was a man of unbounded pride, which, notwithftanding the greatnefs of his abilities, rendered him either a fool or a madman. He likewife defpifed every thing that was not Swedifh.

Never did I undertake any affair with more ardour or better fuccefs : I accomplifhed my purpofe, gained his friendfhip, an unlimited power over his mind, and reftored him to his king and country.

The Pruffian minifter, Count Hertzberg, the fame year, came to Aix la Chapelle : I enjoyed the honour of his fociety and converfation three months, and every where accompanied this great man. To his

libera-

liberality am I indebted, that I can, at prefent, return to my country with honour. —— As often as they read this, let my children remember the reafons I have had for inculcating this gratitude in their infant hearts.

The time I had to fpare was not fpent in idlenefs; I attacked thofe fharpers, in my weekly writings, who attend at Aix la Chapelle and Spa, to plunder both inhabitants and vifitants, under the connivance of the magiftracy: nor are there wanting foreign noblemen, who become the affociates of thefe pefts of fociety. The publication of fuch truths endangered my life from fome of the defperadoes, who, when detected, had nothing more to lofe. How powerful is an innocent life, how great that prefence of mind which confcious virtue infpires, nothing can

more

more fully prove, than that I ftill exift, in defpite of all the attempts of wicked and ignorant monks, and defpicable fharpers.

Though my life was much difturbed, yet do I not repent of my manner of acting: many a youth, many a brave and worthy man have I preferved from deftruction, detained from the gaming table, and perfonally pointed out to them the moft notorious fharpers. This was fo injurious to Spa that the bifhop of Liege, himfelf, who enjoys a tax of forty per. cent. on all their winnings, and therefore protects fuch villains, offered me an annual penfion of five hundred guineas, if I would not come to Spa; or three per cent. on the winnings, would I but affociate myfelf with Colonel N——t, and raife recruits for the gaming table. My anfwer may eafily be imagined, yet,

for

for this, was I threatened to be ex-communicated by the holy catholic church.

I and my family paffed the great-eft part of fixteen fummers in Spa. My houfe became the rendezvous of the beft and moft refpectable part of the company, and I perfonally known to fome of the moft worthy people in Europe.

Through life it has been my con-ftant defire to act for the benefit of others, and to obtain juftice for the whole world, as well as for myfelf. Fatal experience has convinced me how vifionary fuch fchemes are. — By an effort of this kind I gave my-felf new caufe of uneafinefs.

A conteft arofe between the town of Aix la Chapelle, and Baron Blan-kart, the mafter of the hounds to the Elector Palatine: it originated in a difpute concerning precedence,

be-

between the before-mentioned wife of the recorder, Geyer (who was, at this time, miftrefs to Baron Blankart, and alfo to a young canon of the church), and the fifter of the Burgomafter of Aix la Chapelle, Kahr, who governed that town with oriental defpotifm.

This quarrel was highly detrimental to the town, and to the Elector Palatine; but, at the fame time, highly profitable to Kahr, whofe office it was to protect the rights of the town, as well as to thofe perfons who were deputed to defend the claims of the Elector: the latter kept a Pharaoh bank, the plunder of which had before enriched the town; and the former, Kahr, under pretence of defending their caufe, embezzled the money of the people: fo that both parties, inftead of wifhing to end, endeavoured, with

all

all their power, to prolong the litigation.

It vexed me to the heart to see
their proceedings. Thofe who fuffered, on each fide, were deceived;
and I conceived the vain project of
expofing the truth, and obliging
thefe difhoneft agents to an accom-
modation. For this purpofe I jour-
neyed to the electoral court, at Manheim, related the facts to the Elector, produced a plan of accommo-
dation, which he approved, and obtained full powers to act as arbitrator.
The minifter of the Elector, Bekkers,
pretended highly to approve my
honeft zeal, conducted me himfelf to
an audience, made me dine at his
houfe, took me to the opera, faid a
commiffion was made out for my
fon, and forwarded to Aix la Chapelle, which was a falfity, and, the

mo-

moment he quitted me, fent poft to Aix la Chapelle, thereby to fruftrate the very attempt he pretended fo much to applaud. He was, himfelf, in league with the parties. In fine, this honeft, but filly, interference in what did not concern me, brought me only trouble, expence, and chagrin. I made five ineffectual journies to Manheim, till at length I became fo diffatisfied that I determined to quit Aix la Chapelle, and purchafe an eftate in Auftria, where I might live in philofophic eafe, and purfue the innocent avocations of agriculture.

The Bavarian conteft was at this time in agitation : my own affairs brought me to Paris, and here I learned particular intelligence of great confequence : this I communicated to the Great Duke of Florence, on my return to Vienna.

The

The Duke departed to join the army in Bohemia, and I had occasion again to write to him, and, from the importance of the subject, thought it my duty to send a courier, at my own expence. The Duke shewed my letter to the Emperor; my intelligence was received, but I myself remained unnoticed.

I did not think myself very safe, in foreign countries, during the time of war, and therefore purchased the lordship of Zwerbach, with appurtenances, which, with the concomitant expences, cost me sixty thousand florins. This lordship was in a ruinous condition, and was to be restored by my money and industry.

To conclude this purchase, I was obliged, at great expence, to solicit, during eleven months, the referendary, Zetto, whose present habitation is the house of correction, and his good

P 6   friend

friend whom he had appointed as my curator, and my new estate was, likewise, made a *Fidei commissum*, for my kind referendaries and curators would not let me escape contribution. The six thousand florins, however, of which, in one year, they exonerated my purse, would have done my family much service.

In May, 1780, I went to Aix la Chapelle, where my wife's mother died, in July, and, in September, my wife, myself, and family, all came to Vienna.

My wife solicited the mistress of the ceremonies, to obtain an audience. Her request was granted; and she had the good fortune to gain the entire approbation and favour of the Empress. Her kindness was beyond expression: she, herself, introduced my wife to the Arch-Dutchess, as an example for

women,

women, and commanded her grand miſtreſs of the ceremonies to pre-ſent her every where. " You were " unwilling," ſaid ſhe, " to accom-" pany your huſband into my coun-" try, but I hope to convince you that " you may live happier in Auſtria, " than at Aix la Chapelle." She ſaid many other things equally kind.

She next day ſent me her decree, aſſuring me of a penſion of four hundred florins, adding this ſhould not be all ſhe would do for me.

My wife petitioned the Empreſs to grant me an audience; her requeſt was complied with, and the Empreſs ſaid to me, " This is the third time in which " I would have made your fortune, " had you been ſo diſpoſed." The audience laſted long; her diſcourſe was that of a matron. She deſired to ſee my children, adding, " So ex-" cellent a mother muſt have brought " you

" you charming children." She then spoke of my writings. " How " much good might you do," said she, " would you but write in the " caufe of religion !"

The profpect now feemed to brighten, and a happy futurity to approach. My wife received more honour and attention, while fhe remained at Vienna, than many of the firft ladies of the city.

We departed for Zwerbach, where we lived contentedly, but, when about to return to Vienna, and folicit the reftitution of a part of my loft fortune during this momentary funfhine of the court, the great Terefa died, and all my hopes were overcaft.

I forgot to relate that, after my favourable audience, the Arch-Dutchefs, Maria Anna, fpoke to me in the name of the Emprefs, and defired

fired me to tranflate a religious work, written in French, by the Abbé Baudrand, into German. I replied, I fhould have little fuccefs in tranflation, but that I would obey her majefty's commands. I began my work, took paffages from Baudrand, but inferted more of my own, though the cenfor was lefs faftidious in the examination of what was intitled a tranflation. The firft volume was finifhed in fix weeks; the Emprefs thought it admirable. The fecond foon followed, and I prefented this myfelf. She afked me if it equalled the firft : I anfwered, I hoped it would be found more excellent. "No," faid fhe, " I never in my life " read a better book;" and added, fhe much wondered how I could write fo well and fo quick. I promifed another volume within a month.

Before the third was ready, Te-refa

refa died, and my expectations defcended with her to the grave. She continually gave orders, on her death bed, to have the writings of Baron Trenck read to her; and, though her confeffor well knew the injuftice that had been done me, and all I had loft, yet, in thefe her laft moments, when he had the moft favourable of all opportunities, he kept a daftardly filence, though he had given me his. facred promife to fpeak in my behalf.

The cenfor permitted me, after her death, and the Arch-Dutchefs even commanded that I fhould print what I have here ftated in the preface to that third volume, and this was my only fatisfaction.

Untoward, indeed, has ever been my fate. For one and thirty years had I been foliciting my right, which I never could obtain, becaufe the
Emprefs

Emprefs was deceived by wicked men, and believed me an arch-heretic. In the thirty-fecond, my wife had the good fortune to convince her this was falfe; fhe had determined to make me reftitution, and my children fortunate, and juft at this moment fhe died.

Oh Fortune, how doft thou fport with the paffions of men! Yet, was it not fo much the fault of fortune, as of myfelf. I was at length humble enough to accept juftice as a favour, but then it was too late. My heart was confcious of not needing favour or forgivenefs, for I had never done ill, therefore did I continue unfortunate; I chofe the narrow path of innocence, my enemies the open field of vice. Their ftation was the ftrongeft, and they have kept poffeffion. All conteft is now paft, I am too old, and need reft.

For

For my children's fake have I written this hiftory, have told thefe open truths, which, perhaps, may draw down new perfecution on my head. The friends of innocence will be their friends. I have taught them to live fatisfied, in this world, with what is neceffary, and without what is fuperfluous. Be this their inheritance, inftead of their great Sclavonian eftates; for the reft, I leave it to God, and that good fame in which their forefathers have always lived.

The penfion granted my wife, by the Emprefs, in confequence of my misfortunes, and our numerous family, we only enjoyed nine months. This fhe was deprived of by the new monarch, who fuppreffed that, and various other penfions, as burthenfome to the ftate. He, perhaps, knew nothing of the affair, as I never foli-

folicited. Yet, much has it griev-
ed me. Perhaps I may find relief
when the fighs wrung from me fhall
reach the heart of the father of his
people, in this my laft writing. At
prefent, nothing for me remains, but
to live, unknown, and buried, in
Zwerbach.

After the death of the Emprefs,
that I might fulfil every duty to my
family, I wrote to the Emperor, defirous to be fully informed of what
I had to hope. This was my memorial.

" Moft Gracious Emperor,

" In a work printed at Aix la
" Chapelle, in 1772, the moft effen-
" tial parts of which I had the ho-
" nour to prefent to you, in 1765, in
" manufcript, is the following paf-
" fage :

' All oppreffed fubjects ought, at
' ftated

' ſtated hours, to have acceſs to the
' throne; thoſe who ſhould prefer
' falſe complaints, ſeek to deceive, or
' obtain favours unmerited, ought
' to be made public examples, and
' ſtand mutilated in the pillory.'

" I, moſt gracious Sovereign, am
" the firſt who will pronounce judg-
" ment on myſelf, if I am not able
" to prove I have been moſt un-
" juſtly oppreſſed under the reign
" of the great Maria Tereſa, and
" deprived of an immenſe property
" by unjuſt judges, and men in
" power : I, therefore, humbly pray
" a judge may be appointed, before
" whom I may be permitted to pro-
" duce my proofs.

" I am,

" Gracious Monarch,

" Your ever faithful ſubject,

" TRENCK."

In

In vain did I hope an anfwer: my petition remained unnoticed, unregarded.

The Emperor thought proper to collect the legacies, and monies, beftowed on hofpitals, into one fund. The fyftem was wife and good. My coufin Trenck, as I have before faid, had bequeathed thirty-fix thoufand florins to a hofpital for the poor of Bavaria; who had been ruined by him, and his pandours. This I fhewed he had no right to do, having deducted the fum from the family eftates ; I, therefore, petitioned the Emperor that thefe thirty fix thoufand florins might be reftored, as by right they ought, to me and my children, who were the people whom 'Trenck had indeed made poor, nothing of the property of his acquiring having been left to pay this legacy, but, on the contrary,

the

the money having been violently exacted from mine.

Alas ! The memorial came before thofe who were ill informed of the truth, or deemed the enquiry too laborious. In a few days it was determined I fhould be anfwered in the fame tone in which, for fix and thirty years paft, all my petitions and remonftrances had been anfwered:

THE REQUEST OF THE PETITIONER CANNOT BE GRANTED.

Fortune, my irreconcileable enemy, perfecuted me even in my retreat. Within fix years, two deftructive hailftorms fwept away my crops; one year was a mifgrowth; there were feven floods; a rot among my fheep; all poffible calamities befel me, and my manor.

The eftate had been totally ruined,

the

the ponds were to drain, the man-
fion-houfe to repair, three farms
were to be put into a proper condition, and the whole new ftocked.
This rendered me poor, efpecially
as my wife's fortune had been funken
it law-fuits at Aix la Chapelle and
Cologne.

The unfortunate, miferable peafants had nothing, therefore, nothing
could pay ; I, on the contrary, was
obliged to advance them money.
My fons affifted me ; and we laboured with our own hands: my wife,
accuftomed to the affluence of the
great world, anxious to fulfil the
duties of a mother, and an excellent
woman, took care of eight children,
without fo much as the help of a
maid. We lived in poverty and
wretchednefs, obliged to earn our
daily bread by the fweat of the brow;
and, had the Emperor, by chance,

amid his peregrinations, vifited Zwerbach, he would have beheld the abode of induftry and virtue, exerting themfelves to fulfil all the duties of man, and our fufferings had certainly been lefs fevere.

Enough : I have aided myfelf. The monarch, who oppreffed, never beheld me crouching to his power. I have deferved a fate more favourable; I avoided a place where men are not actuated by the love of men, and hid myfelf in my Zwerbach : I fighed, faid nothing, wrote much, feared no man, and rather defired to feek the world's utmoft boundaries, than live a witnefs of certain fcenes.

The greateft of all my misfortunes was my treatment in the military court, where Zetto and Krügel were my referendaries. Zetto had clogged me with a curator, and, when the

cow

cow had no more milk to give, they then began to torture me with deputations, fequeſtrations, adminiſtrations, and executions. Nineteen times was I obliged, perſonally, to attend in Vienna within two years, and to travel fourteen poſts each time at my own expence. This alone ate up my income. Every ſix years muſt I pay an attorney to diſpute, wrangle, and quarrel, in my behalf, with the curator. Their mutual ſquabbles filled huge rolls of writing, for all of which I, in the concluſion, was obliged to pay. If any affair was to be expedited, I, by a third hand, was obliged to ſend the referendary ſome excellent ducats. Did he give judgment ſtill that judgment lay fourteen months inefficient, and, when it then appeared, the copy was falſe, and ſo was ſent to the upper courts, the high refer-

endary of which said " I muſt be
" diſlodged from Zwerbach."

True it is, no ſuch ſentence was
ever inſerted in their proceedings,
and, probably, he in turn may be
diſlodged himſelf from the ſeat of
judgment, and once more become
the companion of the honourable
Zetto, in the houſe of correction.
So ſhall his power be loſt, to diſ-
lodge, to baniſh, worthy citizens
from the territories of Auſtria.

They obliged me at laſt to pur-
chaſe my naturalization. I ſent to
Pruſſia for my pedigree, where the family had been known four hundred
years; the atteſtation of this was ſent
me by Count Hertzberg. Although
the family of Trenck had a hundred
years been land-holders in Hungary,
yet was my attorney, by order of the
court, obliged to ſolicit the inſtru-
ment called ritter-diploma, for

which, under pain of execution, I must pay two thousand florins. Thus are men treated in Vienna, and this treatment I, certainly, shall not soon forget.

By decree, a Prussian nobleman, is not noble in Austria! In Austria! Where every lackey, every worthless fellow, can purchase a diploma, making him a knight of the empire, for twelve hundred wretched florins!. Where money is the only merit necessary for acquiring the title of Count! Where such men as P—— and Graffalkowitz have purchased the dignity of PRINCE!

I am, at length, suffered to be at rest. They, by whom I was persecuted, instead of cleansing courts of justice, cleanse the streets. They may, perhaps, soon have company.

Tortured by courts, terrified by hail-storms, I determined to dread

them

them no more, determined to depend on the productions of my pen, and to publish a collection of my works in eight volumes, and this hiftory of my life.

Fourteen months accomplished this purpofe. My labours found a favourable reception through all Germany, procured me money, efteem, and honour, and I will now no more ftruggle through my few remaining years under the burthen of law-fuits, curators, referendaries, attornies, courts of juftice, and the unworthy in authority. I will live as if I never had poffeffed any property on this poor earth but what is included within my own head. By my writings only will I feek the means of exiftence; by my writings only endeavour to obtain the approbation and the love of men.

For this I need not be of any

coun-

country, want no title, no protection, no court favour, no lordfhips,
no particular place of abode, no uniform, no *Fidei commiff-curator!* I am
a free burger of the world, depend-
ent on no earthly prince; and to
my children I will leave my literary
property. This nothing can con-
fifcate.

* * * * * * * * * *

On the 22d of Auguft, 1786, the
news arrived that Frederic the Great
had left this world!

* * * * * * * * * *

The prefent reigning monarch,
the beft among the friends of men,
the witnefs of my fufferings in my
native country, immediately fent me
a royal paffport for Berlin. The con-
fifcation of my eftates was annulled,
and my deceafed brother, in Pruffia,
had left my children his heirs!

* * * * * * * * * *

I jour-

I journey, with the imperial permiffion, back to my country, which I have been two and forty years expelled! I journey — not as a pardoned malefactor, but as a man whofe innocence has been eftablifhed by the whole tenor of his actions, has been proved in his writings, and who is journeying to receive his reward!

Here I fhall once more encounter my old friends, my relations, and thofe who have known me in the day of my affliction. Here fhall I appear, not as my country's Traitor, but, as my country's Martyr! The Martyr of Virtue!

What is the expanfion of my foul at obtaining that for which I fo long have laboured! What my joy at the profpect of futurity, at the victory which fortitude, honour, and truth, unfhaken, have won! I

ima-

imagined my end would have been, what my life was—tragical! But a different scene opens to my view. Of this resplendent scene again shall I appear one, and now have I to prove I am the very man I have so often asserted myself to be, in this my history. Yet is it a great under-taking for a grey head, become grey in its contests with misfortune, and requiring retirement and rest. Slumbering ambition, lulled by philoso-phy, again is roused, animates and inspires my soul, prompting me to seek that reward for others which, once, I sought for myself. To them I leave my name and rights; to them whom, not requiring their consent, I called into existence; who, from the example of their fa-ther, contemplating the past, might imagine this nether world only the hell of man, and that they must

first

firſt expeƈt the rewards of virtue beyond the grave, had they not learned, from my example, alſo, to expeƈt better of futurity. Yes, for my eight children will I ſtill live; them will I conduƈt into thoſe paths of honour in which I was, myſelf, conduƈted by my anceſtors: paths to me ſo gloomy, yet ſo glorious.

Safe am I arrived in haven, a weather-beaten, but experienced, ſhipman, enabled to indicate the hidden rocks and quickſands of this life's perturbed ſhores; often have I ſtruck, often been wrecked, but ne-ver foundered.

Poſſible, though little probable, are ſtill future ſtorms. For theſe, alſo, am I prepared. Long had I reaſon daily to curſe the riſing ſun, and, ſetting, to behold it with hor-ror. Death to me appears the greateſt benefit; a certain paſſage

from

from agitation to peace, from motion to reft. I fear not the terrific
dreams of futurity. My children,
however, jocund in youth, delight
in prefent exiftence. When I have
fulfilled the duties of a father, then
may I voluntarily ceafe to live; nor
is it impoffible but a remarkable
fupplement may follow, of the ftrange
viciffitudes of this my life, in which
I may fpeak more openly of things
I have been, in prudence, obliged
partly to conceal.

Thou, oh God! my righteous
judge, didft ordain that I fhould be,
that I might remain, an example of
fuffering to the world; thou madeft
me what I am, gaveft me thefe
ftrong paffions, thefe quick nerves,
this univerfal glow, this thrilling of
the blood, when I behold injuftice.
Strong was my mind, that deeply it
might meditate on deep fubjects;

ftrong

ftrong my memory, that thefe meditations I might retain; ftrong my
body, that proudly it might fupport
all it has pleafed thee to inflict.

Could I believe, with St. Paul,
there are, indeed, veffels of wrath
fitted for deftruction, then might I
affirm that, to fuch, this world were
a hell. But not fo: with the eyes
of philofophy I contemplate the
good God, who, himfelf, is void of
wrath, revenge, or the poor paffions
by which his poor creatures are tortured. Him have I to thank for
enabling me to encounter and to
conquer a hoft of troubles, and leaving me ftill in being to reap the
fruit of my victories.

Should I continue to exift, fhould
identity go with me, and I fhould
know what I was, then, when I was
called Trenck; when that combination of particles, which Nature commanded

manded fhould compofe this body,
fhall be decompofed, fcattered, or
in other bodies united; when I have
no mufcles to act, no brain to think,
no retina on which pictures can
mechanically be painted, my eyes
wafted, and no tongue remaining to
pronounce the Creator's name, fhould
I ftill behold a Creator; then, oh
then, will my fpirit mount, and in-
dubitably affociate with the fpirits
of the juft, that expectant wait their
golden harps, and glorious crowns,
from the moft high God——For
human weakneffes, human feelings,
arifing from our nature, fpringing
from our temperament, which the
Creator has ordained fhall be even
thus, and no otherwife; for thefe
have I fuffered enough on earth; for
thefe can I have nothing to fear,
beyond the grave, from a juft God,
who made me man, and not angel,.
and

and ftationed me in that world in which his own hand had mingled good and evil.

Such is my confeffion of faith: in this have I lived, in this will I die. The duties of a man, and of a Chriftian, I have fulfilled ; nay, often have exceeded, often have been too benevolent, too generous ; perhaps, alfo, too proud, too vain; I could not bend, although liable to be bro-ken. Many a fleeplefs night has a noble thirft of knowledge made me pafs. Exiftence was given man to be employed — I fhall have fleep enough in eternal night.

That I have not ferved the world, in acts and employments where beft I might, is, perhaps, my own fault; the fault of my manner, which is now too radical to be cor-rected, in this my fixtieth year. — Yes, I acknowledge my failing, ac-
know-

knowledge it unblufhingly; nay, glory in the pride of a noble nature. Joy fhall fpring up and quicken in my heart, when my example, the in-ftructions I give to youth, fhall teach them, idle and thoughtlefs as they often are, virtue and wifdom, and thus enfure their happinefs. Joy fhall make my white locks again youthful, when grey beards fhall learn, from me, to think and act more honourably, and to die tran-quilly. Joy fhall again enlighten my foul, when the deceitful fhall become honeft; the idle induftrious; the ignorant learned; the flave a free man; and the man of fin, upright, juft, and benevolent.

For myfelf, I afk nothing of thofe who, having read my hiftory, fhall become my friends, for nothing I need; but to them do I commit my wife and children. My eldeft fon

is

is a lieutenant in the Tuscany regiment of cavalry, under General Lascy, and does honour to his father's principles. The second serves his present Prussian majesty, as ensign in the Posadowsky dragoons, with equal promise. The third is still a child. — My daughters will make worthy men happy, for virtue and gentleness have they imbibed with their mother's milk. Monarchs may hereafter remember what I have suffered, what I have lost, and what is due to my ashes. With this reflection I calmly quit the world.

Here do I publicly declare —— I will seek no other revenge against my enemies than that of despising their evil deeds. It is my wish, and shall be my endeavour, difficult as is the task, to forget the past, and, having committed no offence, neither will I solicit monarchs for fa-

vour

vour and pofts of honour, but, as I have lived a free man, a free man will I die.

Let the wife and benevolent reader grant me compaffion, and, by my example, avoid much of that mifery in which too much rafhnefs, or too little caution, has involved me.

He, whofe untimely ambition impels him to undertakings beyond his ftrength; he, who concerns himfelf with affairs not properly his own; he, who erects himfelf into a reformer of this world's abufes, will be the martyr of virtue, or, perhaps, the dupe of folly, and, after having lived perfecuted, may even have the fortune to die defpifed.

I conclude this my hiftory on the evening preceding my journey to Berlin: now, when I take leave of my beloved wife and children. Grant, oh God, that for them I may journey! God

grant

grant I may encounter no new afflictions, to be inferted in the third
volume of this tragical hiftory.———
Higher and better be my hopes.

Dated at the Caftle of Zwerbach,
    December 18th, 1786.

TRENCK.

END OF VOL. II.